AF225707

Also by Bud Fussell
From Indigo Sea Press

Destiny

Mixed Emotions

Redemption

Scoundrel

Second Chances

Serenity

Shepherds

That One Night

Towers

Whirlwind

To Paradise and Back

indigoseapress@gmail.com

Saving
San Sorento

By

Bud Fussell

Deep Indigo Books
Published by Indigo Sea Press
Winston-Salem

Deep Indigo Books
Indigo Sea Press
302 Ricks Drive
Winston-Salem, NC 27103

For information regarding bulk purchases of this book, digital purchase and special discounts, please contact the publisher at indigoseapress@gmail.com

Cover design by Pan Morelli
Manufactured in the United States of America
ISBN 978-1-63066-571-5

Chapter One

From the first time Monty Shepherd invited Jerry Martin to go with him on a speaking trip to one of the Fellowship of Christian Athletes banquets, the two had been friends. Now, that they've been on a number of trips together, they are best friends. Monty had retired as owner and chief executive of the huge Shepherd Global Apparel Company, and Jerry retired from his duties as owner of the very successful Martin General Contracting Company, in Douglasville, Georgia, and was currently, partner in the internationally known Thomas–Martin Developers.

Before he retired, Monty had his beautiful Florida beachfront property enlarged, and once, when Jerry and Tracy were their guests, Jerry made a deal to buy the large property next door to Monty's that had a tremendous amount of beachfront. Although Monty lived in Chattanooga, Tennessee and Jerry in Douglasville, Georgia, they were next door neighbors in Florida, and each spent about fifty percent of their time down there.

Joan, Monty's wife, and Tracy, Jerry's wife had become very good friends, also, and even though Monty and Jerry were not there, sometimes, Monty would send one of the Shepherd planes to deliver the two ladies to Florida and then return to pick them up and take them home.

Recently, Joan had read about a seldom heard of place described as a tropical paradise, named San Sorento. She and Monty researched it and decided that it would be a really neat place to go. Surprisingly, there were several top-notch hotels, and it sounded as if it was just the right place for a vacation. Joan called Tracy and told her about it, and after talking to Monty about it, she invited her and Jerry to go with them. It sounded good to Jerry, so they set up a date to go. They would fly Shepherd Apparel's big 767 for the ultimate in comfort.

San Sorento was a Spanish speaking island nation of approximately one million people, located between the main country of Mexico and the peninsula of Baja California. It was around two thousand miles from Chattanooga.

San Sorento is run by a Presidential form of government. The President has most of the power, but he is checked by a Legislature to keep him or her from gaining too much power. San Sorento has been operated this way for decades and most of the population seems to be satisfied with it.

The big Shepherd plane landed safely at the San Sorento airport, and the Holiday Shores Hotel, where they had a reservation, had a shuttle bus that ran from the hotel to the airport, and Monty and Jerry and their wives took it to the hotel. The two pilots, Alex and Cody would catch it later, after they had secured the plane.

The hotel was one beautiful place. Spacious

rooms, exceptional bathrooms, comfortable beds, and not only were their rooms on the ocean, but their view was unbelievable as well. Joan told Monty, "Honey, I don't know why we haven't been here before. This place is beautiful."

Monty said, "We haven't been here before because we didn't know this place was here. I don't know how you found it."

The next day was a typical day at the beach, and then, on the second day, something happened that would change things.

After a pleasant morning on the beach, the two couples went up to their rooms to get ready to go get some lunch. The lady at the desk had told them about a place that served American type food, such as hamburgers, hot dogs, and fries, so they decided to go there, since they would be eating the local fare at dinner.

They were just about ready, and Monty was putting the final touches on his hair, when there was a loud knock on the door. Joan was already ready, so she looked through the peep hole in the door and saw a man standing outside. She didn't answer it, but instead hollered for Monty and said, "Honey, a man knocked on the door, and he's standing outside. Do you want to get it?"

He came in from the bathroom and opened the door and asked, "Hi. Can I help you?"

The man said, "I certainly hope so, sir. My name is Bimo Flores, and I am the president of San Sorento

Clothing Manufacturing Company. Are you Mr. Shepherd?"

"Yes. I'm Monty Shepherd. How did you know I was here?"

"I was at the airport and saw your beautiful airplane, and after asking around, I found out your name. Mr. Shepherd, I have a business proposal that I think you might be interested in."

"Well, Mr. Flores, I don't think I would be interested in any business propositions down here. You see, all my business dealings are in Chattanooga, Tennessee, and I wouldn't be interested in anything away from Tennessee."

"I understand, Mr. Shepherd, but if you will give me just ten minutes to explain what I want to tell you, if you don't like what I'm going to tell you, I will leave, and you won't see me again. May I have ten minutes?"

The man looked sincere and almost desperate, and not wanting to hurt his feelings, Monty said, "Okay. Ten minutes, but that's all. My wife and our friends are getting ready to go to lunch. Tell me about your proposition."

"Thank you so much, Mr. Shepherd. I'll tell you quickly. About twenty-three years ago, a man who owned a large sales agency in Mexico City went to see our president, President Putra, with an idea about starting a clothing manufacturing company here in San Sorento. He told President Putra that he had a designer that could design clothes so popular that it would take a large factory to produce it all, and that he and two other agencies that he was in cahoots with could take all the production.

"After much negotiating and investigating, President Putra decided to go along with the man because our local economy was hurting and people needed the jobs. We, and I'm including myself, built a large state-of-the-art factory and began production twenty years ago, and true to his word, they kept our factory operating at capacity until the designer died about three years ago, and we haven't had a designer since then. All we have been able to do is to produce older styles, and the Agency in Mexico City says they cannot continue to buy the older styles and if we can't get an up to date designer, then they will have to quit buying from us. If they quit buying from us, Mr. Shepherd, then we will have to completely go out of business. We had almost five hundred employees before this happened, and now, we are down to around fifty, and that's temporary.

"Now, here is my proposition to you. If you would be willing to come in here and take over our business, we would be willing to furnish you with the building, the warehouse, all our machines and cutting equipment, and everything else at no charge to you. Also, the sales agency in Mexico City said they would buy all our production if it suited them. As you Americans say, this is our offer to you in a nutshell. What do you think, Mr. Shepherd?"

"Your offer is very interesting, Mr. Flores, but I'm

not the only one you have to talk to. You see, I retired a while back and I made my son the president of our company, and he is in charge of our day-to-day operations. I can't make a decision like this. It would have to go through my son, Jimmy. I'll tell you what I'll do. You show me your building and machines and other equipment tomorrow, and if I like what I see, I'll talk to my son about it. Does that make sense to you?"

"Yes sir. That would be wonderful. I can show you this afternoon if you would like.:

"No. I'm here on vacation with friends, and I don't want to get bogged down in some business deal. Tomorrow is fine, and I would like for my friend to see the building. He is a famous builder in the United States, and he can tell me about the quality of the building and warehouse. Is that a problem for you?"

"No, no. No problem. Would ten o'clock tomorrow morning suit you?"

"Yes. Ten o'clock will be fine. Will you pick us up?"

"Yes. I'll pick you up, and Mr. Shepherd, would you mind calling me Bimo?

I don't like Mr. Flores."

"Yeah, Bimo, and I'm Monty, okay?"

"Okay, Monty. Thank you, and Monty, would you have time tomorrow to meet President Putra?"

"I don't think so on this trip. If I like what I see tomorrow and if my son wants to pursue this, we'll have to come back, and there will be plenty of time to meet him, okay?"

"Okay. I'll look forward to next time."

Bimo was right on time the next morning, and he took them through a part of town that looked as though it was depressed. Then, all at once, there was a magnificent looking building, with a sign over the front entrance that said in Spanish, *Empressa De Ropa San Sorento,* which Monty guessed meant San Sorento Clothing Company. He was very impressed with the building as was Jerry, who he had asked to go with him to see the company. They walked around outside before they went in, and the lawn area was impeccable, with the grass mowed and shrubs trimmed. Monty complimented Bimo on keeping the place looking so nice, and then they went in. The office area was very nicely laid out, and when they got into the plant itself, Monty recognized it as a typical clothing manufacturing plant, and the few people that were working seemed to be keeping their minds on their work.

He asked Bimo, "How many square feet are in this building?"

Bimo said, "One hundred and fifty thousand."

Monty whistled and said, "That's what I was thinking. This is about the same size as some of our plants in Chattanooga. Do you have any warehouse space?"

"Yes sir. We have a nice warehouse in back of this building. "

"How large is it?"

"It has sixty thousand square feet in it."

"That's a nice sized warehouse. Was it adequate for your needs?"

"Yes sir. We used the cloth and stuff up almost as soon as we got it in, so we didn't need to warehouse it for very long."

"How did most of your raw materials come in?"

"Mostly by forty-foot containers, and sometimes by air cargo airplanes."

Monty said, "Off hand, I don't know too much about shipping costs, but it seems to me that by the time you ship something by containers and all the distance it has to travel, shipping by containers would be too expensive. A container would have to go all the way down the coast of the United States and then down the coast of Mexico to the Panama Canal, and then all the back up the coast of Mexico to San Sorento. That would be extremely expensive. That's something we'd have to think carefully about. It would probably be cheaper to ship the goods to Hawaii than to San Sorento."

Bimo could see that his hopes were slipping away, and he said, "Yes, it was expensive, but we usually received ten, forty-foot containers at a time, and the shipping company said they were giving us a reduced rate, so it was cheaper than if we had received containers one at a time."

"Yeah, but that reduced rate was probably not nearly enough to make it worthwhile to ship large quantities by container that distance."

The whole time that Monty and Bimo were talking

and looking over things, Jerry was inspecting the building, and he was satisfied that the building was very well built.

After they had finished going over the plant building, they walked out back to look at the warehouse. Due to the company's lack of business, the warehouse didn't have very much in it, but Monty and Jerry could easily see that it was built for efficiency. Monty noticed that they had a forklift, and he wondered if that was enough to unload containers and then load and unload the goods at the warehouse. He thought to himself that they should probably have at least three.

When they finished at the warehouse, Monty told Bimo, "Bimo, I liked what I saw, and as I told you, if I liked it, I would talk to my son about it, since he is our current president. I'll be going home Saturday, and I'll talk to him no later than next Monday. I'll call you and let you know what he says whether it's good or bad. If he thinks it's a good move to come down here, we'll have to come back and do a tremendous amount of preliminary work before we can even think about reviving the plant. Those are the promises I made to you, and I hope you're satisfied with what I've done, so far. I can tell you this; I liked what I saw, and maybe, after I talk to Jimmy, something will develop. Now, if you don't mind, Bimo, take Jerry and me back to our hotel before our wives put out a search party for us."

Monty and Jerry didn't talk at all about what they had seen on the way back to the hotel, but after they got back, Monty stopped in the lobby and asked Jerry, "What did you think of those buildings? Are they any good?"

"Yeah, they're quality built buildings, Monty. When I look at a building for inspection purposes, I look for the little things to see if the builder included them as they should, and those two buildings both had everything I looked for. I don't know what you're going to do, business wise, but if you don't come over here, it shouldn't be because of inferior buildings because those buildings are not inferior. They're top notch."

"Thanks, Jerry. I appreciate that. Boy, look at the time. We had better get back to our wives or they might go to lunch without us."

When they got upstairs to their rooms, their wives had gone down to the beach. Instead of calling, Jerry went next door and knocked. Monty came to the door, and Jerry said, "It looks like our wives got tired of waiting on us and went to the beach. Do you want to go down there or do you want to wait up here for them to come back?"

"Since we've been gone most of the morning, I hate to have to go out for lunch. I think I might just go down to the beach and kick back in a chaise lounge and let the girls go to the dining room here at the hotel and get us some lunch and bring it down to us. That way, we'll already be in position for a nap when we finish, but if you'd rather do something else, we can do whatever you want."

"No, no. I like the way you think. I'll get my suit on and meet you at the beach."

The two couples had a very enjoyable, lazy, hazy day at the beach. They did what Monty had suggested. The girls went to the restaurant at the hotel and picked up lunch and took it down to the beach, where they ate, and then Monty and Jerry took naps in their chaise's while the girls made plans to go to Florida when they got back.

Since they didn't have a car with them, they were sort of limited on what they could do. Of course, they could always take a cab, but their purpose for coming was to relax, and it's hard to relax when you're driving or riding, so they made it a point to do things that didn't require going places. That night, they did get a cab to go to a nice restaurant for dinner, and then they went back to the hotel and played Rook until bedtime.

At nine o'clock the next morning, Monty's phone rang, and when he looked at the caller ID, it was Bimo.

Monty answered and said, "Good morning, Bimo," and even after Monty answered that way, Bimo said, "Good morning, Monty. This is Bimo. Did I wake you up?"

"No, we just got back to our room from eating breakfast. What's up?"

"Bimo, I talked to President Putra yesterday after you and I were together, and he would like to meet you. He wanted me to tell you he is free this morning from ten to eleven o'clock, and he hopes you will come to his office then. Monty, I know you're on vacation, and I hate to ask you, but in this country, when the president wants something, people try to do it. Would you do me the great favor of letting me pick you up and take you to meet the President? Again, I hate to ask you."

"Sure, I'll go with you, Bimo. We sure don't want to get the president mad at you. When will you be here?"

"Is nine thirty alright with you?"

"Yeah, that will be fine. I'll be downstairs."

"I'm very grateful, Monty. "I'll see you at nine thirty."

Monty went to the bathroom and brushed his teeth and then caught the elevator to take him down to the lobby, and he hadn't much more than got down there until he saw Bimo pull up. He went out and got into the van, and they headed to the President's headquarters.

Bimo pulled into a VIP parking place, and they went in. The interior was like what you'd see in a movie. After a couple of minutes, a uniformed man came out and said, "Mr. Shepherd, the President will see you now."

He and Bimo got up and followed the man to a very large, plush office. A handsome, distinguished gentleman met them as they went in and said, "Mr. Shepherd. I'm President Arin Putra. It's nice to meet you. Good morning, Bimo. You gentlemen have a seat."

Monty replied, "Thank you, Mr. President. It's nice to meet you, also."

The president asked, "What do you think of San Sorento?"

"I think it's beautiful. This is my first time here."

"Bimo tells me that you said you might bring your company here to San Sorento."

"That's not exactly what I said. I told Bimo that although I am CEO of Shepherd Apparel, I am actually retired, and when I retired, I made my son President of the company. I agreed to let Bimo show me your company, and I told him that if I liked what I saw, then I would talk to my son about it. I did like what I saw and as I promised Bimo, I'm going to talk to my son about it as soon as I get home, but the decision is going to have to be his."

"When are you going home, Mr. Shepherd?"

"We're planning to leave Saturday, Mr. President."

"And you will talk to your son when you get home?"

"Yes sir, and I'll call Bimo next Monday one way or the other."

"Did Bimo tell you what we are willing to do for you if you come?"

"Yes sir. He told me some of the things, but I'm curious as to how long the contract between us would last. You see, if we should decide to come to San Sorento, it will cost us a lot of money, and a short-term contract wouldn't be worth it."

"How long do you think the contract would be for?"

"Mr. President, I would rather you tell me."

President Putra smiled and asked, "Is forever long enough?"

Monty smiled back and said, "Yes sir. I think forever would be good."

The president said, "Seriously, we would entertain a ninety-nine-year lease, if that would interest you."

"Mr. President, this conversation just keeps on getting better. Are you serious?"

"I'm completely serious."

"What would Shepherd Apparel have to do to get a ninety-nine-year contract?"

"Nothing. Just keep our people working."

"You know, Mr. President, my father told me one time that if someone offers you something that looks too good to be true, it probably is, and this looks too good to be true. Is it?"

President Putra said, "Mr. Shepherd, let me say this. You go back to Chattanooga and tell your legal team what we discussed and have them draw up what you call an "iron clad' contract, and then you bring it back down here, and I'll sign it as well as the Chief Representative of our Legislature. Now, does that sound too good to be true?"

"I don't know what to say, Mr. President. You make a very convincing point. I will definitely talk to my son, Jimmy about this when I get home."

"Mr. Shepherd, you said you are the CEO of

Shepherd Apparel, and you made your son president when you retired. From what I know about business, the CEO of a company is higher than the president, and if he really wants something, he can get it. I hope this is the case with Shepherd Apparel. Now, if you'll excuse me, I have another meeting. It has been my pleasure meeting you. Please call Bimo next week and let him know where you and your son are on this matter. I almost forgot this. Bimo, why don't you tell Mr. Shepherd how to get in touch with Jose Martinez? If Jose would want to still buy San Sorento's production, it might make a difference in the decision."

"Thank you, Mr. President. Meeting you has truly been my pleasure. I'll try to call Bimo next Monday."

Chapter Two

On the way back to the hotel, Monty said, "Tell me about Jose. The president seemed to think it's important."

"Oh yeah. I was going to tell you about him. He's the one who got San Sorento Clothing started in the first place. He's the one who knew the designer that designed all our clothes for twenty years, and his company and two other sales companies bought all our production for all that time."

Monty asked, "When were you going to tell me all this? If this guy would like to buy all of San Sorento's production, this could make a difference in our decision. The president was right about that. I'm surprised that you didn't tell me about him. How about getting me his number? I'd like to talk to him."

"Okay. I'll get you his number just as soon as I get back to my office."

Bimo took Monty back to his hotel, and when he got up to the others, he said, "Well, I just got back from meeting the president of San Sorento, and he seems to be a really nice guy. You'll never guess what he offered me."

Joan said, "Offered you? What?"

"He said that if I would bring Shepherd Apparel to San Sorento to revitalize a large clothing plant they have that is in trouble, we could get the plant and warehouse along with all the machinery and equipment at no cost to us, and they would give us a ninety nine year lease at no charge. I've never heard of such a thing, and oh yeah, Bimo is getting me the number of the sales agency that bought all their production for the entire twenty years they were in business. He thinks this guy will want to buy ours if we come down here."

Jerry said, "You're going to take it, aren't you?"

"Well, if it was up to just me, I might would have said I would, but it's not up to me. Jimmy is the president of the company now, and all I can do is tell him about it and leave it up to him."

"You're going to encourage him to do it, though, aren't you, Jerry asked?"

"Well, let's just say that I'm going to tell him about the offer and let him know how excited I feel about it, but the final decision will have to be his. What are you all getting ready to do?"

Joan said. "Nothing, really. We're just about ready to go to the beach. You want to go?"

"Yeah, if you all are going, I am too."

They all went down and took the same chairs and chaises that they had been previously using. They talked about what a good time they were having, and Monty apologized for his interruptions, and just as he was finished apologizing, his phone rang. It was Bimo, and he had Jose Martinez' number.

Monty said, "Bimo, I'm on the beach right now. Can you give me time to get back up to my room and call me back with it in about five or ten minutes? Have you talked to Jose?"

"No, I haven't talked to him in quite a while."

"Bimo, why don't we do this? Why don't you call him right now and tell him what's going on with San Sorento and Shepherd Apparel and tell him I want to call him just as soon as you hang up. If you will do that, I'll be back to my room by the time you finish talking to him, and you can call me with his number, so I can call him. Will you do that?"

"Si. I'll call him right now, then call you back."

"Good man. I'll be listening for your call."

He hurried up to his room to be there when Bimo called him back, but after being in his room for about ten minutes, Bimo hadn't called. Fifteen, eighteen, twenty minutes passed with still no call, and Monty was getting pretty irritated. He decided to go back down to the beach and try to get over his irritation.

When he opened the door to leave, Bimo was standing there with his hand up in position to knock. Monty said in a curt tone, "I thought you were going to call me back in five or ten minutes. What's wrong? Couldn't you get hold of him? I wish you had called me back."

"Oh no. I talked to him, and he is very excited to talk to you. He said I should bring you his number so I could be with you when you two talk. I don't understand, but that's what he wanted me to do. He is waiting for your call right now."

"Okay, and you have his number with you?"

"Si."

"Good. How about you placing the call for me. All these numbers you have to use on international calls are confusing, and you know what these are, so if you don't mind, just call him for me. Before you call him, does he speak English?"

"Si. He speaks very good English."

He then placed the call and handed the phone to Monty. After two rings, Jose answered, "Jose Martinez."

"Hi Jose. This is Monty Shepherd. How are you?"

"I'm fine, Mr. Shepherd. It's nice to talk to you. Bimo says that you may revive the San Sorento Clothing Company. Is that right?"

"Well, Jose, it's too early to tell, but we're talking about it. If we should make the deal, do you have any interest in buying some of our goods?"

"Mr. Shepherd, if you make the right things for us, we can maybe take all your production in San Sorento. When will you begin?"

"Hold on a minute, Jose. We haven't decided yet whether we're going to come in here or not. There are still many questions that have to be answered."

Jose said, "I answered a big one, didn't I?"

"Yes, you did. I wish we could get together and discuss things, man to man."

"When are you leaving San Sorento?"

"Saturday."

"Mr. Shepherd, if you can stay over until Sunday, I can come up there Saturday and we can talk Sunday."

"I can't do that, Jose, and here's why. First of all, the final decision will be up to my son because he's the president of our company, and secondly, we don't do business on Sunday."

"You don't do business on Sunday? Why?"

"Because we believe in God, and God says we should not do any work on Sunday. Do you believe in God, Jose?"

"Yes I do, but I guess I don't obey His rules the way I should. When do you think you and I might get together?"

"I don't know, Jose. I'm going home Saturday and talk to my son about it, and then if he is interested in taking my suggestion, we might come down here next week. Could you come up here next week?"

"If you come, when will you be here?"

"If we come, we'll probably be here on Tuesday. Can you come then?"

"I can probably come on Wednesday. Maybe you and I can talk then."

"Maybe so. I'll know after I talk to my son. How about if I call you Monday and let you know if you should come up here or not. There's one more thing, Jose. Bimo is the one who started this, and I don't want to do anything unless we include him, okay?"

"Okay, Mr. Shepherd. I appreciate your honesty and fairness. I'll be happy to include Bimo."

Monty said, "Well, I guess that's about all we can do today, unless you can think of something else."

"I have nothing else. I will pray all weekend that

you will call on Monday."

"Maybe I can. It was good talking to you, Jose. There's something I'd like for you to do for me in case you come up here, and that's to bring me figures of the last three years before you cut out their production. Can you do that?"

"I can. Goodbye, Mr. Shepherd. Hope to hear from you Monday."

After they hung up, Bimo said, "I heard what you told Jose about including me on everything, and I really appreciate that."

Monty said, "Bimo, my dad taught me to always be fair and honest in my dealings because if I'm not, there's a good chance that God will punish me; maybe not right then, but sometime. Do you believe in God, Bimo?"

"I think so. When I was a little boy, my parents took me to meetings of some kind, but we called him Allah."

"Allah, hunh? Did Allah send his only son to die so you could be saved?"

"If he did, I don't know about it."

"Well God did that and listen to this. He sent his Son to be born unto a virgin, and after He died, He came back to life after three days, and He's alive today. Did Allah do anything like that?"

"I'm not sure. I never heard about it if he did."

"Well, what are some of the things that Allah did?"

"I really don't know, Monty. All I know is that

when I was a young boy, my parents said I should believe in Allah."

"Well, do you?"

"I don't know, Monty. I guess so."

"Maybe we can talk some more about this, later, if you want to. I'd like to tell you what Jesus has done for me."

"I'd like to hear that."

"Okay, Bimo, I'm gonna go back down to the beach to be with my wife and friends. Remember, if Jimmy likes what we've been talking about, we'll probably be here next Tuesday, if that's alright with you, but I'll call you Monday, one way or the other." Friday was the last day of vacation, and they took full advantage of it. Jerry and Monty neither one ever slept late, so they were up early and downstairs drinking coffee before their wives got up. Later, they all had breakfast together and then, it was down to the beach. Lunch was ordered at the hotel restaurant and taken to the beach to eat, and then an afternoon at the beach with a nice dinner at the hotel. That last night, Monty invited Alex Russell and Cody Marvin, his pilots, to join them for dinner. It was a nice cap to an enjoyable vacation, at least for three of them. Monty had so many interruptions that he didn't feel much like he had had a vacation.

Alex ordered food for lunch and an afternoon snack before they took off Saturday morning, and they took off at nine o'clock. The weather was good, and the flight was pleasant, and they reached

Douglasville at four thirty that afternoon.

Tracy and Jerry said their goodbyes and the plane took off for Chattanooga, arriving at Lovell Field at five thirty. Monty had called ahead, and Jimmy was there to meet them.

On the way home, Jimmy asked, "Did you all have a good time?"

Joan said, "It was wonderful," and Monty said, "Yeah, it was good, between interruptions."

"What do you mean?"

"I'll tell you later. It's got me excited, and I hope it will you."

"Well, I can't wait to hear it. When are you going to tell me?"

"I'll tell you after we get back from dinner tonight."

"Oh, that reminds me; Analisa is cooking and she wanted me to tell you all to come to our house for dinner."

Joan said, "That sounds wonderful."

Not much else was said the rest of the way home. Jimmy pulled in Monty's driveway, even though they lived next door to each other, to cut down on the distance when carrying all their bags. Jimmy thought his mother must have taken all the clothes she owned by the number of bags they had. Finally, everything was unloaded and taken in the house, and Jimmy said, as he was backing out of the driveway, "Y'all come on over when you want to. Johnny's anxious to see you, and Dad, I'm anxious to hear what you have to tell me."

"Okay. We'll be there in a few minutes."

Monty was so anxious to talk to Jimmy about San Sorento that he walked over to his house, leaving Joan at home unpacking and hanging up her things. After he hugged Analisa and spent a little time with Johnny, he and Jimmy went into the den, and Jimmy said, "Dad, you're being so mysterious about something in San Sorento that I hope you're ready to tell me what it is."

"I'm not being mysterious. There's just a lot to tell, and I hope you'll be as excited about it as I am."

"Okay, okay. Just tell me."

Okay. The second day we were there, a man knocked on our door, and when I opened it, the man said his name was Bimo Flores, and he was president of San Sorento Clothing Company, that was about to go out of business, and he wondered if maybe Shepherd Apparel might be interested in reviving their business. I told him I was not the one to make that decision; that it was you, and he said, 'Will you at least let me show you our factory,' and I agreed to look at it the next morning, so he picked Jerry and me up the next morning and took us to the factory.

"Son, you wouldn't believe what we saw. It was a large, one hundred and fifty thousand square foot plant with a sixty-five thousand foot warehouse. Inside, it had all practically new sewing machines and up to date cutting equipment. Jerry inspected the buildings while I looked at the machinery and other equipment, and he said they are very high-quality buildings. As he said, 'They are top-notch'.

"Then he made me an offer that blew me away. He said that if we would come to San Sorento, that we could have the building and all the equipment at no charge. They just want us to give their people jobs. When they were really humming, they worked about five hundred people, but most of them are now laid off."

"What happened to their business?" Jimmy asked.

"Well, I think Bimo said that twenty-three years ago a man came to see the President of San Sorento with an idea for a new manufacturing company. This man had a designer that he said was such a good designer, that if they would open a plant and make his designs, that they could keep the plant busy on just those designs. They opened the plant and ran it wide open for twenty years, and then the designer died. Not knowing how or where to find another designer, all they could do was to make the same old styles they were making before the designer died, but the salespeople couldn't continue selling the line without new styles, so they pulled out.

"I talked to the head of their main sales agency yesterday, and he told me that if we would move into San Sorento and make Shepherd Apparel there, that he felt he could buy all our production. I told him would have to talk to you about it and get back to h and I promised him that I would call him Monda

"Then, on Thursday, your daddy had an audi with the President of San Sorento. I wish you have seen me in the President's office."

Jimmy interrupted and said, "I'm sure it was something to behold."

"It was, and the President made me a promise that I almost couldn't refuse."

"What was the offer?"

"He told me to come home and have our legal team draw up an iron clad contract, and he and the Chief of the Legislature would sign it for a length of ninety-nine years.

"Now, a one hundred and fifty thousand square foot plant with all fairly new machines, an already trained sewing room, a sales agency ready to buy all the production, and a free ninety-nine-year lease excites me. Does it you?"

"Dad, you haven't said where the sales agency is."

"Mexico and Central America. Son, there are ut one hundred and seventy-five million people in area, and we don't have anyone there. To me, to San Sorento is a no-brainer, and I hope you e."

laughed and said, "WOW. Dad, I think could drop an atom bomb on your head, uld come up with a pocket full of

nty asked,

an you're excited about it?"

would have to be crazy not to be you talk about it. Of course, I'm

Just then, Analisa called them to supper. They got up and `went to the table, talking on the way. When they sat down and before they started eating, Jimmy asked, "Dad, what's your honest to goodness, gut feeling about this thing?"

Monty said, "I think we should pursue it, and I think you and I should go out there so you can see what I'm talking about."

While he was answering Jimmy's question, Analisa and Joan brought the food, and he continued to talk. Joan said, "Honey, you've got plenty of time to talk after you eat. Analisa worked hard on this meal, so you should stop talking business now and eat your supper.

He stopped talking and said, "Analisa, Honey, I'm sorry. Would you please pass me the green beans? Everything looks delicious. I'm ready for a good, home cooked meal, aren't you, Mama?"

And Joan said, "I sure am."

They finished a very enjoyable meal, and Jimmy and Monty went back into the den where they talked more about the San Sorento thing. Monty asked Jimmy, "Have you got anything real pressing next week?"

"No. Just a regular week, why?"

"I thought you and I might go to San Sorento so you could see why I'm so excited. We could take our wives and they could enjoy that beautiful beach while we work. There are a lot of questions still to be answered, and I just think it would be a good thing if we went. Jose what's his name, the guy that has the sales agency said he could go Wednesday, if we're going to be there, and I told him I'd call him Monday. What do you think?"

"You seem to be so sold on the deal, that I'd be crazy to buck you on this. You have a long, successful track record, and I'm still on my training wheels, so I say let's go."

"Do you want to take Analisa? I know she'd love it. Your mother sure did, and I know she'd like to go back."

"What will we do with Johnny?"

"We could ask Mother if she would let him stay with her. I'll bet they would both like that. Then, he called Joan and Analisa to come there, and when they got into the room, Monty said, "Ladies, it looks like Jimmy and I are going to San Sorento next week, and we thought you might like to go with us. Would you?"

Joan said, "You know I would," and she looked at Analisa and said, "You should go. It's really pretty and so nice."

Analisa said, "But what about Johnny?"

Jimmy said, "Granny Thil would probably like for him to stay with her."

"Well, if she would, then I'd like to go. Which one of you is going to ask her?"

Monty said, "I don't mind asking her."

Analisa asked, "How long will we be gone?"

Monty said, "Three or four days. Maybe a week. We have a lot to do, so it's hard to plan a definite schedule. If Mother keeps Johnny, she won't care how long we're gone."

Joan asked, "When are we leaving?"

"Tuesday morning," Monty said.

For years, Shepherd Apparel had been holding staff meetings the first thing every Monday, and that Monday was no different. Jimmy held the meeting the way he always did. The rest of Monday was going to be a busy day for both Jimmy and Monty. Jimmy had to plan ahead for being gone, and Monty had to talk to Bimo as well as Jose Martinez, to tell them that he and Jimmy would be there the next day. He especially wanted to talk to Jose because his sales could make the difference in whether Shepherd Apparel moved to San Sorento or not.

He attended the staff meeting the way he used to, some of the staff members wondered why he was there, since he was retired, but nobody said anything about it. Everybody seemed glad to see him, and they all came by to speak and shake his hand, making him feel good that he was apparently so well thought of.

To him, the hands on the clock were just dragging after the meeting. He was anxious to make his calls, but the time in Mexico City was an hour behind Chattanooga, and the time in San Sorento was two hours behind. He knew Jimmy was busy, and he didn't want to bother him, so he went to the break room and had a cup of coffee to help pass the time until he could make his calls.

Finally, it was ten o'clock, Chattanooga time, nine

o'clock, Mexico City time, and he felt sure Jose would be at work by then, so he asked Elizabeth Farmer to place the call for him. She was used to making international calls with all the strange numbers, so he felt she wouldn't have any problem calling Jose.

She zipped right through all the numbers and when Jose answered, she said, "."Mr. Martinez, please hold for Monty Shepherd."

Monty picked up the phone and said, "Good morning, Jose."

Jose said, "Good morning, Mr. Shepherd. I didn't think this morning would ever come. I really am glad to hear from you. Have you made a decision about San Sorento?"

"Jose, like I told you last week, the decision will have to be my son's. I talked to him about it when I got home Saturday, and he's interested, but he can't decide anything without seeing the plant and finding out more about it. You said you could go to San Sorento on Wednesday. Can you still do that?"

"Si. Will you be there?"

"Yes. My son and I are going tomorrow, and we'd like to meet you and talk to you. What time do you think you will be there?"

"How about we meet for a late lunch?"

"That sounds good. We'll be with Bimo.so when you get there, just call him and we'll meet you."

"Very good. Mr. Shepherd, I'm very anxious to meet you."

"Me too, Jose. How about bringing the sales figures we talked about the other day? Will you do that?"

"Si, I'll bring lots of figures. I'll see you Wednesday, Mr. Shepherd. Thank you very much."

"You're welcome, Jose. See ya Wednesday. Bye."

He felt good after talking to Jose, and the next thing he had to do was to call Bimo. He had called Bimo before, so he knew how to do it. He dialed the number, and after a few rings, Bimo answered. "Bimo, Monty. Good morning."

"Monty, I'm glad to hear from you. I was afraid you were not going to call."

"I told you I would, didn't I?"

"Yes, but I was still afraid you wouldn't."

"Bimo, let me tell you something. If, and I say if, we're going to work together, you're going to have to learn that when I or my son tell you that we're going to do something, we do it. Okay?"

"Okay, Monty. I'm sorry. Do you have something to tell me?"

"Well, I want to tell you that we'll be there tomorrow."

"With good news?"

"I don't know yet, Bimo, but I can tell you this. My son is interested, but he has to see everything and find out everything. Also, I talked to Jose before I called you, and he is going to be there around lunchtime on Wednesday. You might decide where you want us to eat."

"I don't have to. I know where Jose wants to eat; The Italiano Restaurante. He always wants to eat there."

"Good. We both like Italian. Look, I'd like for Jimmy to see your plant while there are still people working tomorrow afternoon. Do you think you could pick us up at the hotel after we get settled?"

"Si. You and Jimmy come, and I'll take care of you."

They flew in the next morning and took the hotel shuttle from the airport to the hotel. Monty called Bimo and said, "Bimo, Monty. We're at the hotel. Can you come get us?"

"Si. I can get you. I'll be there in fifteen minutes."

"Great. We'll be looking for you. Thanks, Bimo."

In a few minutes, Bimo pulled up, and after Monty introduced him to Jimmy, they left for the plant. As they approached it, Jimmy saw it from the van and asked Monty, "Is that it?"

"That's it," Monty said, and Jimmy said, "Wow. You weren't kidding, were you?"

Bimo pulled into his parking space, and they all got out. Jimmy just stood there for a minute, looking around, and again, he said, "Wow. This is amazing."

Monty said, "It is, isn't it? Let go in."

They went in just like the first time Monty saw it. They entered the office complex first, and then worked their way back to the plant. There were several women and three men operating sewing machines. Jimmy was surprised at the men, and he asked Bimo, "Do you normally have many men running sewing machines?"

"When we're running full force, we have several, but they're laid off now."

They stayed in the sewing room for a little while longer, and then they went into the cutting department. Jimmy paid close attention to the cutting tables, spreaders, and cutting knives. No one was working in the cutting department that day because they didn't have anything to cut. He was impressed with the equipment, though.

From the cutting department, they went into the receiving and shipping department. From what he could tell, they had everything set up in a way to operate efficiently,

From shipping they went out to the warehouse. It was virtually empty, and that made it look twice as large as it actually was. Jimmy noticed a modern looking forklift sitting there.

The whole tour took maybe an hour and a half or two hours, and Bimo said, "Jimmy, this is it. What do you think?"

Jimmy said, "Bimo, it's very nice. It's a shame you don't have enough business to fill it up."

Bimo said, "This is where I hope you and your company will come in. We can make much clothing when we are working."

Monty said, "Thank you Bimo. If you will, you can take us back to our hotel now. I just wanted Jimmy to see what you had. We have our wives with us, and they are tired from our trip, so we'll go eat dinner and go to bed early. What time do you want to pick us up in the morning?"

"Will eight thirty be alright?"

"That's perfect. We'll see you then. Remember, Jose Martinez is coming tomorrow, and I'm looking forward to meeting him."

"I know. I'll pick him up at the airport when he gets in. Would you like to go to the airport with me to pick him up?"

"Yeah. That will be fine."

When they got to the hotel, both ladies were lying on their beds. They were tired from the trip, and Monty suggested that they just eat at the hotel, rather than go out to some restaurant, and that suited everybody, so that's what they did.

Bimo was right on time the next morning. At eight thirty, he drove right under the covered entrance to the hotel. The Shepherds got in and they went straight to Bimo's office, where they talked about the San Sorento Clothing Company. Monty and Jimmy had many questions, and Bimo was able to answer them all.

At eleven thirty, Bimo's phone rang and it was Jose saying he would be there at one fifteen.

The three spent another hour or so in Bimo's office, going over various parts of the business, and then, at about a quarter to one, Bimo said, "We need to go meet Jose now. Are you ready?" They said they were, and they went outside and got in the van for the trip to the airport.

At the airport, they stood at the window in the terminal, looking out on the runway, and in a minute, Bimo said, "Here comes Jose."

Monty asked, "In that white plane?"

"Yes. That's Jose."

Monty was mildly surprised because Jose's plane was a pretty Gulfstream Four, or G4 as it was normally called. He thought to himself, *boy, this guy must really be a power hitter.*

Jose's plane taxied up to its designated parking place, and after doing what he had to do on the plane, a tall, nice-looking, well-groomed man got off and walked to the terminal. Bimo said something to him in Spanish, and then in English, he said, "Jose, I'd like for you to meet Monty Shepherd, and this is his son, Jimmy." They all shook hands and told each other how nice it was to meet, and then Bimo winked at Monty and asked Jose, "Where would you like to eat lunch?"

Jose said, "I think you know where I'd like. The Italiano Restaurante, but if you gentlemen would rather go somewhere else, it will be alright with me."

"No, no," Bimo said, we'll go to the Italiano Restaurante. Monty and Jimmy said they like Italian food," so they all got in the van, and Bimo drove to the Italiano Restaurante.

Jimmy and Monty had old favorites; veal parmesan and lasagna, but Bimo and Jose had dishes that neither one of them was familiar with.

After lunch, they went back to Bimo's office, where Jose and Monty led the conversation. Monty asked, "How large of an area do you cover, Jose?"

"We cover all of Mexico except for three states, and I gave those three to my friend Bruno Chavez, who has Chavez Sales."

"You gave three states to somebody else? What's the population of those three states?"

"Around ten million people."

"You mean you gave away ten million possible customers?"

"Si, but by doing that Bruno and I will each realize more business."

"I don't understand that, but maybe you can explain it to me sometime. What's the population of the area that you didn't give away?"

"Close to one hundred and thirty million."

"What's the population that Bruno covers with the three states that you gave him?"

"Fifty-four million."

"So, you're telling me that between the two of your companies, you are working a population of roughly a hundred and seventy-five million people. Now, do you think Bruno is interested in representing Shepherd Apparel?"

"Oh yes. I talked to him, and he is excited about the possibility."

"Well, what is the total area that he covers?"

"He covers all of Central America plus the three states in Mexico that I gave him."

"Wow. I didn't realize that Central America had that many people."

"Let me ask you this, Jose. When I first began talking to Bimo, he said something about three sales agencies. Where is the other one?"

"He is still in business, but when San Sorento said they were going out of business, he picked up another company to replace them, and we are now covering what he used to cover, and if you take over San Sorento, and if you want us to cover Mexico for you, we can more than likely produce more sales for you in his area than he did."

"Jose, have you ever been to Chattanooga?"

"No. I have only been to Texas two or three times. Why?"

"Well, Chattanooga is in Tennessee, not Texas. The reason I asked is that when we take on a new sales agency, we like for them to come to our headquarters in Chattanooga to see our plants and to learn how we do some things. Now, we haven't signed on with San Sorento yet, but in case we do, will you be able to come to Chattanooga."

"Oh si. I can come to Chattanooga whenever you say."

"Do you think Bruno would come?"

"Si. I could bring him with me. No problem."

"Okay, but as I said, we haven't fully decided on whether to get in bed with San Sorento or not, but if we do, I think we would like for you and Bruno to represent us in Mexico and Central America, don't you, Jimmy?"

Jimmy said, "Yes. Yes, I do."

"I appreciate that, Monty and Jimmy. Do you know when you will decide?"

Monty said, "I hope to this week, while we're here. We have several things to do while we're here, and our legal department is going over what Bimo and President Putra told me to see if things can be worked out. I personally think it would be a win-win situation for all of us if we can make it work. If we come, I still have to come up with answers on how we're going to ship, and especially how we're going to receive goods, and a big problem is how to figure out where we're going to house our employees that we will have to send down here to retrain the new personnel."

Jose asked, "If you decide this week that you're going to, as you say, get in bed with San Sorento, when do you think you would want us to come to Chattanooga?"

"I don't know exactly, Jose. If we decide to do this, we're going to have to come back down here to get the contracts signed and everything else that will have to be done before starting operations. The New York Market comes up in about three weeks, and we have to get ready for that, so there's not much time. Let's see, Jose. It looks as though next week is the only time we will have until after the New York show. What's your schedule for next week?"

"My schedule is to come to Chattanooga, if you want me to."

"That's good because I'll be there next week. I'll

have to come back here week after next, and that will only leave one more week to get ready for New York. Unless I call you to tell you something different, why don't you plan to go to Chattanooga next Wednesday? "Are you and Bruno both married?"

"Yes, we're both married."

"Why don't you plan to bring your wives with you. Do they both speak English?"

"Yes. Very good English."

He smiled and said,

"That's good because our wives don't speak Spanish. I mentioned a while ago about shipping and receiving. When you were taking all of San Sorento's production, how did you get it?"

"By forty-foot containers. Bimo's people would fill the containers and take them to the San Sorento wharf to be put on a freighter. The freighter would take the containers down the Gulf of California to the Pacific Ocean and down to Acapulco, where the containers would be put on trucks and delivered to us. We could save money on freight by having ours and Bruno's shipped to the same place at the same time. Bimo would mark our container Martinez A and Bruno's, Martinez B."

"That sounds like a good system. Did you ever have the containers get switched?"

"Never. The truck line was very good."

"Okay, Jose. Do you have any questions for Jimmy or me?"

"No sir. Not right now. I'm sure I will later. Will

you call and let me know something?"

"I will. I'll call you no later than Saturday of this week. If I don't let you know until Saturday, will that have any bearing on you going to Chattanooga next week?"

"No. I'm going to plan on going, then, if something happens, I can cancel."

Okay. That's all I have. Do you want to ask him anything Jimmy?"

"No. Not right now. If he goes to Chattanooga next week, I'll probably have several questions then."

"Are you spending the night here, Jose?"

"No. I'm going back."

"Man, it's going to be a long day for you."

"That's alright. My pilot has probably been napping ever since we landed, and I don't worry about him. He's used to long trips with me."

"Do you know how to fly?"

"Not really. I fly a lot, and I watch my pilots. I usually have two of them. I've learned enough by watching them that if anything ever happens, I think I could get us on the ground. Bimo, will you take me to the airport?"

Bimo said, "Yes. I'll take you. Monty, do you and Jimmy want to go with us, and I can drop you off at your hotel after we leave the airport?"

Monty said, "That would be good. I think we're through for today, don't you? Oh, do you have any realtors here? We have to find somewhere for our people to stay if we send some of them down here."

"I don't know of any realtors, but I might can find some places for you."

They got to the airport, and Jose got out. They all shook hands and said they hoped to see him in Chattanooga the next week. After the goodbyes, he went out and got on his plane, and they waited and watched it take off.

"He looks like a good man," Monty said.

Bimo said, "He is a good man. If you make the deal with us, you won't have to worry about selling what we make here because he and Bruno will sell it all for you.

On the way to the hotel, Monty told Jimmy, "This looks good, doesn't it? You open a plant and hope you can sell your product, and here, if we open a plant, we've got everything sold before we make it. What do you think about that?"

Jimmy said, "I wouldn't have believed it had I not seen it for myself, and one good thing about it is we aren't in Mexico or Central America either one now. That's a major blessing."

When they arrived at the hotel, Monty told Bimo, "Bimo, tomorrow, I've got to find somewhere for our people to stay when we send them down here. It's going to be a deal breaker if I can't find a place, so rack your brain tonight and hope we can find a place tomorrow."

"Don't worry, Monty, we'll find a place. I'll see you in the morning. Is eight thirty alright?"

"That's good. See you in the morning."

Jimmy and Monty took the elevator upstairs to their rooms, where their wives were waiting for them. They each asked the other about their day and talked about where they would like to have dinner. Jimmy and Analisa walked outside and sat on the patio, while Monty kicked back in a comfortable chair in his room and took a short nap.

Later, they all went to a fairly nice restaurant for dinner, and then returned to the hotel and played Rook until bedtime. While they were playing, Joan said that she and Analisa would like to take a guided tour around San Sorento, and she asked Monty if he would call downstairs to the desk to see if there was anything like that available.

He did and found out there was a place that gave tours, so he booked one for the next day with a lady named Juanita. He was told that she would meet Joan and Analisa at one o'clock the next afternoon in the hotel lobby.

The next morning, Bimo picked Monty and Jimmy up, and the first thing he told them was that he couldn't find any realtors in San Sorento, but then, he said, "I have an idea. It might be too expensive, but maybe you can negotiate."

Jimmy asked, "Where is it?"

"Do you remember seeing a place called the Dunes? It's not too far from here, and it's on the beach. Why don't we look at that?"

"Jimmy said, "I feel sure that will be too expensive for what we want."

"Well, why don't you look at it anyway? Some developers came in here a few years ago and built it as a first-class resort, thinking it would stay full all the time, and at first, it was busy all the time, but for the last year or so, it hasn't had much business, and the word is they're going to have to close down, unless business picks up."

"Monty said, "I don't see that we have much choice. Let's go look at it and see what they say because if we can't get it, then we may not be able to close the deal between Shepherd and San Sorento. Bimo, I'm going to ask God to help us get it. Do you think it would help if you asked Allah to help, too?"

Before they left to go up there, Monty said, "Bimo, before you start the motor, sit here for a minute. Jimmy and I are going to pray and ask God to help us if He thinks the Dunes is the right thing for us. Monty bowed his head and said a short prayer out loud. Jimmy bowed, too, and said a silent prayer, asking the same thing, and Bimo didn't know what to do. He sat there and watched Monty as he prayed and watched Jimmy with his head bowed. Monty concluded his prayer with, "In Jesus name I ask this, Father," and then he raised his head as did Jimmy, and said, "Okay Bimo, let's go to the Dunes and see what happens."

It was only a couple of blocks from the hotel up the beach to the Dunes Resort. When they got out of the car and before they went in, they walked around the resort just to see what it was like. It was very impressive, with a really nice pool. It had shuffleboard, horseshoe pits, and other things to do outside. Bimo had told them that it had over one hundred one- and two-bedroom efficiencies. There were a few three-bedroom units on the top floor. They went in and asked to see the manager, but the lady at the check-in desk said the manager was not there. He had gone fishing.

She couldn't speak English, so all the questions Monty had, had to go through Bimo. He told Bimo to tell her they were interested in renting several units and could they go in and see two or three. She agreed and gave them the keys to three units.

They went to the first one and unlocked the door and went in, and Jimmy said, "Dad, this is really nice. Don't you think so?"

The unit had a kitchen with a range, refrigerator, dishwasher, and microwave. It had a generous supply of cooking utensils and dishes. The apartment had a nice sized living and dining room combination, one bedroom, and one bathroom. There was a deck running across the living room and bedroom. Plenty of room for one or two people.

He asked when the manager would be in, and she said the next morning. He asked the prices for a group rate, and she didn't know if they had group rates. He decided that she didn't know much about the place other than what she needed to know as a desk clerk, so he told Bimo to thank her and to leave the manager a message that they would be back the next day.

After drawing a blank at the Dunes, Monty asked Bimo to drive them around San Sorento to see if they might just accidentally run upon something that might work, but after about an hour or more, with no luck, they went to a little place and ate some tacos.

Monty said, "Bimo, I hate to waste the afternoon, but not knowing whether or not we're going to be able to get the Dunes, I don't know anything else we can do. Why don't you take Jimmy and me back to our hotel, and we'll just get a running start on tomorrow."

Bimo said, "Okay, I'll take you. Monty, are you worried about getting the Dunes?"

"No, I'm not worried, Bimo. You heard me ask God for His help, and I'm convinced that I'll get it, so I'm not worried at all. If we don't get the Dunes and can't make the deal with you guys, then I'm satisfied that I've done all I can do, and it's not God's will that we make it, but we still have tomorrow to work on it, so I think I'm going to go sit down at the beach this afternoon. What time did the lady at the Dunes say the manager will be in in the morning?"

"No later than ten o'clock."

"Okay then, why don't you pick us up at ten in the morning, and we'll see what happens when we get to the Dunes."

Bimo smiled and said, "Monty, you're something else. Do you know that?"

"I'll take that as a compliment, Bimo. Thank you."

When they got up to their rooms, the women had

gone on their tour, so they went out and sat by the pool.

About three thirty they decided to go upstairs and take a power nap, and when they got into the lobby, they met Joan and Analisa coming in from their tour. While they waited for the elevator and then on their way upstairs, they asked how the tour was, and was Juanita a good tour guide.

Joan said, "The tour was alright, but the guide was not Juanita; it was a guy named Juan, and I hope I never see him again."

Monty asked, "Why? What did he do?"

"Nothing out of the way, actually. He just didn't know much about guiding. I was very put out with him because he totally ignored me and devoted all his attention to Analisa. If he wanted to tell us something, he looked totally at Analisa and told her. When we got out of the van, he always helped Analisa and was very slow removing his hand from her hand or her arm. I don't think either one of us needed help in anything we did, but he always managed to put his hands on her, someway."

Monty, with a big smile on his face asked Joan, "What's the matter, Sweetie? Are you jealous?"

She had a look on her face when he asked that like she could deck him, and she said, "Certainly not. That idiot was just so unprofessional that I resented his behavior. He made Analisa uncomfortable, too, because she said so." Then she said, "Am I jealous? Humph."

She cooled off in a few minutes, and each couple went to their rooms. The guys were alright, but the ladies were tired, so they decided to have dinner at the hotel. At dinner, Monty said, mainly to Joan and Analisa, "In the morning, we have an important hurdle to jump, and hopefully, we can clear it, but if we don't we'll probably go home tomorrow afternoon, so be prepared for that, just in case."

At ten o'clock, the next morning, Bimo was right on time, as usual, and they went straight to the Dunes Resort. The same young lady was behind the desk, and Monty told Bimo to ask for the manager, which he did. She went behind a wall, which Monty guessed hid the offices, and in a minute, a nice-looking young man came out from behind the wall. In Spanish, he asked, "May I help you?"

Monty told Bimo to ask the man if he could speak English, and the man said he could, in very good English.

Monty stepped up and told the man, "I'm Monty Shepherd."

The man said, "Hi. Monty. I'm Pablo Sanchez. What can I do for you this morning?"

"Pablo, may I call you Pablo?"

"Yes, please call me Pablo."

"Okay, Pablo. This is my son, Jimmy, and this is Bimo Flores. My son and I operate the Shepherd Global Apparel Company in Chattanooga, Tennessee. We are in the top five in the world, manufacturing men's and ladies' sportswear. As you probably know, the San Sorento Clothing Manufacturing Company is on the verge of going out of business, and we at Shepherd Apparel are interested, possibly in taking over the San Sorento Company. If we do take over, we're going to have to send several of our people from Chattanooga down here to retrain current and new employees at the San Sorento plant, and these people are going to have to have a place to live, while they're down here. That's where you come in.

"We're going to be sending approximately sixty people for a period of maybe six months. Your one-bedroom efficiency units would be perfect for our people, and we would not need any maid service. We would, however, want to have the bed and bath linens laundered once a week, and we would pay for that separately. What do you think you could rent sixty units for six months for?"

"Monty, in our high season, our units rent for three thousand dollars a week, American and for the off season, they rent for twenty-five hundred and twenty dollars per week. That's three hundred and sixty dollars a day. Since our business is kind of slow right now, I can probably drop the rent to around two hundred dollars a day."

"Pablo, remember now, this is for sixty people for six months, and we can't pay that much. It looks as though you have hardly any business right now, and anything you can get would help. You know, my dad told me one time that a little bit of something is better than a hundred percent of nothing, and it looks like you're running on a hundred percent of nothing. I'll tell you what we'll do, and this will help you as much as it will us. We'll pay you one hundred dollars per week per unit for sixty units plus laundry, and we'll pay you fifteen dollars a week for each unit's laundry. How about it?"

"Monty, I couldn't even think about renting you our units for one hundred dollars a week. I'm sorry."

Monty said, "Pablo, think about this. Our people will be here during your off season, and when people see over half your resort rented during the off season, you know you're going to fill up when the high season gets here." He did some figuring on his telephone calculator and said, "We'll send you a check every week for six thousand and nine hundred dollars, and I believe that's a lot more than you're getting right now. Do you want to do that?"

"I'm sorry. I would really like to have your sixty people here, but there's just no way I can rent our units for one hundred dollars a week. I'm sorry."

Monty said, "I'm sorry, too. Thank you, anyway, and he said to Jimmy and Bimo, "Let's go."

AS they started to leave, Pablo said, "Monty, wait just a minute. If you will pay twenty dollars for the laundry, I'll accept your offer."

"That's great. I'll pay you twenty dollars," and after figuring on his calculator, he said, "That will make your check seven thousand and two hundred dollars a week."

Pablo asked, "When will it start?"

"I'm not sure, exactly. It will be in about three weeks. Pablo, will you sign a contract, saying you agree to this?"

"Yes. I'll sign a contract."

Monty said, "Very good. I'll try to have it here this afternoon. Will you be here?"

"Yes. I'll be here."

"Great, we'll go now and see you this afternoon."

On the way to the van, Monty asked Bimo if he knew any lawyer that could do a rush job on a contract, and Bimo said, "We can go to the president's office, and I Know some of the people there that can probably do it. Do you want to go out there?"

"Sure, anywhere you say. We've just got to get a contract typed up and signed. The people in the president's office should know how to do what we want."

Bimo really turned it on driving to the president's office, and as soon as they got there, he told the receptionist what he wanted, and in a couple of minutes, a really nice-looking lady came out and spoke to them In English and asked what she could do for them. Monty told her, and she wrote down the details as he gave them to her, and when he was finished, she turned to leave and said, "This won't take long. I'll be right back."

While they waited, Monty asked Bimo, "Bimo, why don't you see if we can get an appointment with the president tomorrow? When we get this contract with the Dunes signed, we'll be almost ready to become Shepherd Apparel at San Sorento."

Bimo got up and went somewhere to talk to somebody, and in a few minutes, he came back and said, "Eleven o'clock tomorrow morning. Okay?"

Monty said, "Okay."

In less than an hour, the nice lady came back out with the typed contract in her hand. She handed it to Monty and said, "Here's what you asked for. You might want to read it, just to make sure it's right, and he did.

He read it carefully and said, "It looks really good, and everything seems to be correct. Thank you so much. You're a lifesaver."

She said, "You're welcome."

They went to the van, and Bimo drove as fast back to the Dunes as he did from the Dunes to the president's office. When they got there, all three of them jumped out of the van and almost ran to the office. When they got inside, the lady knew why they were there, and she went back to get Pablo without them having to ask.

Monty showed him the agreement, and after he read it, he signed it and handed it back to Monty. Then, Monty gave him a copy for his records. As they were leaving, Monty thanked him, and told him he would be back in touch through Bimo.

When they got back to the van and sat down inside, Monty let out a huge sigh of relief and said,

"Man, am I glad to get this because without it, I don't know if we could make everything work or not." Then he looked up and said, "Thank you, God. You are so good, and Lord, please help Bimo realize what you did, so he will know how you work with your people, and how good You are. Thank you again, Lord. Amen."

Chapter Three

After they left the Dunes, Monty told Bimo to take them back to his office. When they got there, he and Jimmy began to plan how to set the plant and office up, and what would they need for Bimo to do to help them. In a little while, they stopped and asked Bimo to take them back to their hotel.

Such a load was taken off their shoulders with the signing of the Dunes agreement that Monty wanted to relax the rest of the afternoon, and take everyone, including Alex and Cody to a nice restaurant that night to celebrate.

When they got to the hotel and went out to sit by the pool, Jimmy said, "Dad, you're unbelievable. Do you know that?"

"What do you mean?"

"Well, a lot of things, but the way you handled that Dunes deal was amazing. I wouldn't have had the courage to ask Pablo to let us rent those nice apartments for a hundred dollars a week. That was unbelievable."

"Well, it worked, didn't it?"

"It sure did work. I think if I ever try to get into something where I have to negotiate, I'm going to call you."

Monty smiled and said, "Well, if you do, it'll probably cost you."

That evening, they all went to a nice restaurant and had dinner, and Monty told Alex and Cody what they had been doing in San Sorento. Cody said, "We've been wondering what's going on. Now we know. It sounds like it's a big deal," and Jimmy said, "Yeah, it's a big deal. A really big deal. Guess who Dad and I have an appointment with in the morning."

"Who?"

"The president of San Sorento."

"You're kidding. The president of San Sorento? No, you don't."

"Yes, we do. How's that for a big deal?"

Cody said, "Man. Alex, we're working for celebrities. Did you know that?"

Alex said, "Maybe we should ask for a raise."

Monty said, "We're not that big a celebrity."

They kidded a little more, and then Jimmy said, "Is everybody about ready? I need to get back to fix my face and get my beauty sleep. I don't want to disappoint the president in the morning."

Cody said, "Oh brother."

Bimo picked them up the next morning in time to reach the president's office for their eleven o'clock appointment.

When the president's assistant came out for them, they all followed him into the president's office. When they entered his office, President Putra said, "Good morning, Monty. Who's this you've got here?"

"Good morning, Mr. President. Mr. President, this

is my son, Jimmy. Jimmy, say hello to President Putra."

"Good morning, Mr. President," Jimmy said. "It's nice to meet you."

After the greetings to the Shepherd men, President Putra said, "Good morning, Bimo," and Bimo said, "Good morning, Mr. President."

The president said, "I hope you gentlemen are bearing good news this morning. Are you?"

Each man was waiting on another to say something, and finally, Monty said, "Yes sir, Mr. President. We think we have just about everything ready to begin revitalizing the San Sorento Clothing Company. We still have a lot to do, but we think we have cleared the major hurdles."

"When do you plan to start?"

"We hope to in about three weeks."

"Wonderful. Are you happy, Bimo?"

"Yes sir. I'm extremely happy."

"I appreciate you coming to tell me this good news. I'll try to be there when you start production, and if there is anything I can do for you, please let me know or have Bimo let me know."

"Thank you, Mr. President. Jimmy and I will be back, probably week after next to get you and your Chief of Legislature to sign the lease, and then we can start shipping raw materials in."

"Well, thank you, Gentlemen, for coming by to bring me this good news. I hope we'll become good friends as well as business associates." His assistant understood that was the end of the appointment, so he escorted them out.

On the way back to the hotel, Monty said, "Bimo, don't forget the papers I asked you to get for me, and I didn't tell you this, but I would like for you to send me a list of all your employees, from when you were running full force up until now., and if there are any that you terminated, include them, but mark them some way. You won't have to pick us up in the morning. We'll catch the hotel's limo to the airport."

"What time do you plan to leave? asked Bimo.

"We're going to take off at nine o'clock. That way, we can be home in time for dinner."

"Monty, would it be possible for me to go to the airport early and get on your plane? It's so pretty, I'd love to get on it, and maybe go through it. Do you think I could do that?"

"Absolutely. You be at the airport at nine o'clock, and I'll take you on a tour."

As soon as they reached the hotel, Monty called Alex and told him to be ready to take off at nine o'clock the next morning, and to order food for lunch and an afternoon snack. Then, he said. Alex, make that nine fifteen. I'm going to let Bimo get on the plane at nine o'clock and show him around, and that will take about fifteen minutes. I think we're going to eat dinner at the hotel dining room tonight, in case you and Cody would like to join us."

"I'll ask Cody. I'd like to. What time?"

"About six thirty."

"Okay. We'll probably see you then."

The next morning, Alex and Cody caught the limo early in order to get to the airport and check out the plane before takeoff, and then the others went later and arrived at the airport at eight fifty. Bimo was already there because he wanted to be sure to get on the plane.

When they got inside, Bimo couldn't believe what he was seeing. Monty took him around, showing him the comfortable furniture, the area where they watch movies, the galley and eating area, the two bedrooms, and the cockpit, or flight deck, where the crew works. After a while, Monty said, Bimo, you're going to have to get off now. We're getting ready to takeoff. You can get back on it sometime later when we're here."

"Okay, Monty. Thank you so much. I hope you have a nice flight home."

"Bimo, be sure to send me those lists I wanted showing the employees."

"I'll go to the office right now and get all that together. You might have it by the time you get home."

"Good man."

He got off and went into the terminal and stayed by the window until they took off, wishing that someday he could ride on that beautiful plane.

At nine ten, they taxied down the runway, and precisely at nine fifteen, they lifted off. Bimo waved to them, but of course, they couldn't see him.

After they got to altitude, Jimmy and Monty moved over to the eating area, and sat at the table. Monty poured himself a cup of coffee, and Jimmy opened a Coke, and then they talked. "Son, I'm trying to think of the best way to ship goods to San Sorento, and every time I think I have a good idea, a C-130 airplane comes back to my mind. Have you thought anything about that?"

"I have, and the only thing I can think about is shipping by containers, and I know you've thought about that, too."

"We're not going to be able to decide anything until we get back to the office, so there's no use trying. I'll contact some freight people Monday, and maybe they can help us decide. In the meantime, what are your thoughts about our new adventure?"

Jimmy said, "I think we made the right move. I don't think we're going to know how much volume it's going to mean to us until Jose and Bruno have the line for six to eight months, but I think we did right. It will be interesting to see what our overhead is going to be. Most of it will be labor and freight."

"We might as well not try to figure out anything, sitting in an airplane. We'll get on it first thing, when we get back to the office on Monday. In the meantime, we need to enjoy today and tomorrow while we're not working."

The rest of the flight was uneventful. Joan and Analisa read, while Jimmy and Monty watched a movie. They all broke for lunch, and the ladies returned to their books, but the guys kicked back in a recliner and took a nap. About two hours out of Chattanooga, Monty called Thil and told her when they would be landing, and asked if she could pick them up at the airport.

The plane landed at Lovell Field at five forty-two, and Thil picked them up in Jimmy's big, good looking Suburban. Johnny was with her, and he was very happy to see Analisa and Jimmy.

On the way home, they stopped at the Ole Smoke House for some good barbeque. Even Johnny liked it. After they finished, they all went to Thil's for a summary of their trip.

The next day, Sunday, was church and then an afternoon of rest.

On Monday morning, Jimmy and Monty were at the office early. Jimmy presided over the weekly staff meeting while Monty talked to some freight haulers about the best way to move large amounts of goods from Chattanooga to San Sorento.

After a lot of careful figuring, Monty called the Mid-Atlantic Aeronautics Company, and asked to speak to someone in sales. In a few seconds, a man answered, "Good morning. Rick Garland. May I help you?"

Monty said, "Good morning, Rick. Are you related to Eugene Garland?"

"Eugene was my dad. Who is this?"

"This is Monty Shepherd. I bought some airplanes from you dad, and I'd like to see if you might be able to help me on another one."

"What are you looking for, Mr. Shepherd."

"Maybe a C-130. Do you know where any are?"

"I'm sure I can probably locate one for you. When do you need it?"

"If I get one, I need it, like today."

"Mr. Shepherd, we don't have any C-130's, but we do have something else you might like. Would it be possible for me to come to your office a little later today?"

"What is it, Rick?"

"Are you familiar with Airbus?"

"Only by name."

"If you will allow me to show you some brochures, I can bring them to your office."

"Can you be here around eleven forty-five?"

"I can."

"Well, you come at eleven forty-five, and we'll go to lunch together, and you can show me what you've got when we get back to my office."

"Sounds good. I'll see you at eleven forty-five."

When Rick arrived, he and Monty went to Tomlinson's for lunch. Monty always liked it there because it was quiet, the food was good, and you could talk without having to yell like in some restaurants.

They spent some quality time, just getting acquainted. Monty had bought some of their other planes from Rick's dad, and he wanted to see if he was as good a man as his dad. It didn't take long for him to find out that Rick was every bit the man his dad was. They finished eating and then went back to Monty's office.

When they got to his office, he offered Rick the chance to use his office restroom, which he declined, so Monty told him to have a seat, while he went to the little boy's room.

While he was in there, Rick went into his briefcase and took out a whole stack of papers and pictures. When Monty returned from the restroom, Rick began talking. He said, "Mr. Shepherd, when you called this morning, you said you were interested in a Lockheed C-130 Cargo plane, and I told you I would look for one. Then I asked you if you were familiar with the Airbus, and you said you weren't. Well, here's a picture of the Airbus A400M, and this is a picture of the Lockheed Hercules C-130E."

"They look a lot alike, don't they?"

"Yes sir, they do, but that's the end of their likeness. The Airbus can carry eighty-one thousand, six hundred pounds, twice as much as the C-130, which can only carry forty-two thousand pounds. It can fly faster and higher, and the only drawback I can see is the range is less than the C-130. How far will you be flying your loads, Mr. Shepherd?"

"First of all, call me Monty, will you, Rick?" and Rick said, "Yes sir, Monty." Now how far will we be flying our loads? We'll be hauling them approximately two thousand miles, each way. What's the range of the Airbus?"

"According to the literature I have, the range is eighteen hundred nautical miles."

"What's the range for the C-130?"

"It looks like it's range is almost twenty-four hundred nautical miles."

"What's the new cost of the Airbus?

"A hundred and eighty million dollars."

"How about the C-130?"

"Ninety-five and a half million?"

"Where is the Airbus made?"

"In Europe."

"So what you're telling me is the Airbus flies slightly higher and faster, and can carry more pounds than the C-130, and it costs twice as much, and it's not even American made."

"Yes sir. I guess that's what I'm saying."

"Well, first of all, Rick, we don't need something that can carry eighty-one thousand pounds. We'll probably be carrying thirty-five to thirty-eight thousand pounds, tops. If the Airbus only has a range of eighteen hundred miles, that means we would have to land and refuel before we got to our destination. It doesn't matter to me if the Airbus can fly higher. I don't care about that. I do care that the foreign made plane costs twice as much as the American made plane. I think the C-130 is what we want to stick with. Were you able to find one?"

"Not this morning, but I did find that a C-130 J is about to come on the market, It's in Florida, and has been parked for almost five years. If we can get it at a price you can live with, it will be the perfect plane for your needs."

"When will you know when and if it will be coming on the market?"

"Probably by the end of this week or no later than next week."

"I hope you can. I'll be here the rest of this week, but I'll be gone part of next week and all of the following week. How about pushing whoever you have to push to get some information this week. If we don't get a plane, then we'll just have to use forty-foot containers, and I really don't want to have to do that."

"Okay, Monty," he said as he was getting up. "I'll make some calls when I get back to my office and let you know what I know."

"Will you be the one getting the listing?"

"No sir. It will probably be someone in Florida, since that's where the plane is."

"Well, if someone else lists it, can you still sell it?"

"Yes sir. It's sort of like Multiple Listings, in real estate. When a house goes on the market, everybody on Multiple Listings has a chance to sell it. That's the way it is with airplanes."

"Stay on it, will you Rick?"

"Yes sir, I sure will."

The balance of Monday and the first part of Tuesday was taken up with going over the lists of employees that Bimo had sent. He had X'd out three or four for reasons known only to him and approved the others. He called Bimo and told him what he had done, and he told him to call all of the ones on the lists except the ones he had X'd out and ask them if they would like to come back to work, and then, after he had rehired all he could from the lists, to start hiring new people until he reached around five hundred people. He asked Bimo, "When you were running full force, how many people did you have working in the office?"

Bimo said, "We had five ladies."

"That's about what I figured we'd need. Are those five on your list?"

"No sir. I thought you were only interested in plant employees."

"I'm interested in all the employees. Did you have an office manager?"

"We didn't have anyone with that title, but we had one lady that sort of kept up with what the others were doing."

"Was she good?"

"Yes sir. Very good."

"Did she know how to do the jobs the others were doing?"

"Yes sir. She taught all of them."

"Do you think you can get her to come back?"

"I don't know. I can try. Monty, office help is hard to find in San Sorento, and if a good office worker gets laid off or wants to switch jobs, they can easily find something else."

"Do you think the five that you had have found new jobs?"

"I don't know. I can call them and see."

"If they haven't, hire them, and tell the one that you said taught the others, that she will be a supervisor. She will be the office manager. Maybe that will tempt her to come back."

"We're going to need office help when we begin, Bimo. Please see what you can do, will you?"

"While I have you on the phone, how many forklifts do you have?"

"We have one."

"Do you have any pallet jacks?"

"I think we have two pallet jacks."

"Is there anything else you can think of?"

"Yeah, Monty, we need two or three hand trucks. We had some, but they disappeared."

"Okay, we'll get some. One final thing. Bimo, we need a plant manager, and I hope you can find one. I prefer a man, but a woman will do if she knows how to handle people.

"Here's our plan, now. Jose and Bruno are coming here on Wednesday and will be here until Thursday. Then, Jimmy and I will be coming back to San Sorento next week to get the president and the chief of the Legislature to sign the lease.

"I'm looking for an airplane, and if I can find one, we'll begin shipping cloth and other stuff to you week after next. If I can't find one, we'll still begin shipping cloth week after next, but we'll have to ship by containers and that will take longer. Can you think of anything else?"

"No sir. Not right now, but if I do, I'll call you.

Chapter Four

At eleven fifteen, the next day, Monty's phone rang, and it was Jose. "Monty, Jose. Good morning. We are about two hours from Chattanooga and should land at one o'clock. Would you be able to have someone meet us?"

"Absolutely. I'll be there myself. Will you be here for lunch?"

"No. We'll have lunch on the plane but thank you."

"You're welcome. Jose, how many pilots are with you, one or two?"

"Two."

"Okay, I made reservations for you and Bruno and your wives at the Holiday Inn, and I'll get rooms for your pilots, too. I'll meet you, and your pilots can take the hotel limousine, okay?"

"That's great, Monty. Thank you so much."

At one o'clock, Monty was at the airport, and at one ten, Jose's G4 landed and taxied up to the terminal. Monty went out to meet them and when they deplaned, Jose introduced Monty to his wife, Lavisa, and then to Bruno Chavez and his wife, Lupe.

They loaded their bags in the Suburban, and before they started up, Monty asked, "What's the plan? Do you gentlemen want to go to Shepherd Apparel and would you ladies like to go to the hotel and then meet up for dinner, or do all of you want to go to Shepherd Apparel?"

Lavisa said in perfect English, "I think Lupe and I would like to go to our hotel, and then meet you later for dinner. Your wife will go with us, yes?"

"Yes, she will go with us as well as my son, Jimmy and his wife."

He took them to the Holiday Inn, and he had already registered them, so all they had to do was sign the registration papers and get their keys.

When they turned into the entrance of Shepherd Apparel, Jose said, "Mama Mia. Look at that, Bruno," and Bruno said, "I second that. Mama Mia."

Monty took them in and began introducing them, beginning with Elizabeth, Jimmy's assistant, and then he introduced Bruno to Jimmy. They went past several offices and then they went into Jeff Ellis' office where Monty introduced him as Shepherd's Sales Manager for the United States. They talked for a few minutes, and then they went to Bryce Coleman's office where Monty introduced him as their International Sales Manager.

Bryce showed the guys a few styles that were really good sellers in different countries, especially in Brazil and South America because he felt that Mexico and Central America might like the same things. They had a very good visit and learned a lot about the clothing that Shepherd Apparel made, and all at once it was five o'clock and Elizabeth and others stopped by to say goodnight.

Jimmy asked, "Dad, what time is our dinner appointment? Shouldn't we leave, so we can go home and get ready?"

"Man. Is it that time already? Absolutely, we need to leave. There are two beautiful ladies over at the Holiday Inn, waiting on these guys, and our wives will whip us if we're late. Time flies when you're having fun, doesn't it?"

Reservations were at The Loft for seven o'clock, and since there were eight of them, they drove two cars. Jose and Lavisa with Monty and Joan, and Bruno and Lupe with Jimmy and Analisa.

When they got there, the Valet took each car and parked them, and when they went in, the maître-d' showed them to their table immediately; a table with a beautiful view of the Tennessee River. The maître-d' had made name cards for each one and had them on the table. Lavisa was next to Monty, Lupe, next to Jimmy, Joan next to Jose, and Analisa sat next to Bruno. That arrangement made it easier for everybody to engage in the conversation without anyone being left out. It also made it easier to get acquainted with the ones they had only met. It was easy to see why he was the maître-d', instead of just a waiter.

Monty took the lead when ordering. He asked everyone if they liked shrimp cocktail, and they all said they did. Then he told them that the Loft had really good steaks, and he suggested the prime rib or the filet mignon. All the men said they wanted the prime rib, and the ladies said they didn't think they could eat that much, so they all went for the filet.

He gave the waiter their order and told him to ask everyone how they wanted their steaks cooked. When he got the information from everybody, he disappeared, and in a few minutes reappeared with eight luscious shrimp cocktails. During the appetizers, they all talked and began to enjoy getting acquainted. Jimmy, Monty, and their wives purposely made it a point to get acquainted with each person, personally, and not even mention business the whole evening.

Everyone was too full for dessert, so they sat at their table for a good while after they finished eating and just talked. Finally, after they had been there for almost three hours, Monty decided they should leave. He and Jimmy delivered their guests back to the Holiday Inn, told them how much they enjoyed the evening and each other and promised to pick them up at nine o'clock the next morning for a tour of the entire Shepherd Apparel campus.

The next morning, Jimmy and Monty picked up the Martinez' and the Chavez' and took them to Shepherd Apparel. When Monty turned into the entrance, Lavisa said, "Oh my goodness."

They took them to the main plant, first, and since the other plants were basically the same, they just went to them, but didn't go through a detailed tour. While it didn't really concern Jose or Bruno at that point, Monty wanted them to see the sock plant, and they spent quite a bit of time there.

When they left the sock plant, Monty took them back to his office, and when they walked in, Elizabeth stopped Monty and gave him a note and said, "Monty, a fellow name Rick Garland called and wants you to call him back. He said it was important."

Monty excused himself from the others and went into Jimmy's office and called Rick. When Rick answered, he said, "Rick, this is Monty. Do you have some good news for me?"

"Monty, hi. Yes sir, I do. That plane I told you about the other day, the one in Florida, has just been listed, and if you're interested in it, we need to move in a hurry. Can I come to your office?"

"Rick, I've got some out-of-town people here right now, but I'm fixing to take them to the airport. Can you come at two o'clock?"

"Yes sir. I'll see you at two."

He went back in his office to discuss some more sales things with Jose and Bruno, and while there, he mentioned the New York Market, coming up in two weeks. Both Jose and Bruno said they were going, mainly to get more familiar with the Shepherd line, and when they said that, Monty told them that if they wanted to, they could fly to Chattanooga and fly to New York with him and his crew on the 767, and that would save him having to fly his plane almost two thousand miles, and Jose jumped at that chance, so they set date and time, and that finished their visit to Chattanooga. Before they took them to the airport, Jimmy asked if they wanted to eat lunch first, and

Jose said, "No. thank you, Jimmy. I told my pilot to have food brought to my airplane, and we will eat lunch in a little while, somewhere over the Gulf of Mexico at thirty or thirty-five thousand feet.

They said goodbye at the airport, and on the way back to the office, they stopped by the Krystal, and both got a sack full of hamburgers to take to the office for lunch. In the car, Jimmy asked, "What did Rick Garland want? Has he found us a plane?"

"Maybe. He told me about one in Florida when I saw him last week, and he called to say it's just been listed, and we need to move in a hurry. He's coming by the office at two o'clock. Are you going to be busy then?"

"I'll make it a point to not be."

Rick was a little early, and Monty and Jimmy were both free, so they had him come on in. They were in Monty's office, and he told Rick, "Tell me about this plane. Do you think it's what I want?"

"Based on what you told me last week, I think it is. It's a two thousand and two C-130J, and it has been parked for the past five years. It has a relatively low number of landings, and it's in perfect shape. It also has thirty-six passenger seats with it, and that's rare."

"How much is it, Rick?"

"Keep in mind that this is almost a hundred-million-dollar airplane with very little usage. The owner is asking eight million dollars, and Monty, I think that's a bargain."

"Rick, I read about one over the weekend that was older, but they are asking only two point seven million for it. It has been my understanding, that age really doesn't affect an airplane as long as it has been taken care of, and that one was supposedly babied all its life. What do you think this guy will take for this one?"

"I really don't know. We can ask him. Maybe seven. Monty, I failed to tell you, this C-130J has the new six blade propeller. I'm pretty sure that older plane you're talking about has three blades, and those three extra blades make quite a bit of difference. Also, Monty, the old C-130's require a crew of five, and this plane only requires a crew of three.

"Tell you what, Rick. Call the man and tell him I'll give him five million cash, if he can get it up here in the next two days. And if he says he'll take the five, ask him if he knows where I can find two pilots and a Loadmaster. We might can make a package deal."

"Okay, I'll tell him. If he won't take five, will you be willing to come up any?"

"See what he says and let me know."

"Okay. I'll try to get back to you this afternoon, but if I can't reach the owner, it will probably be tomorrow."

"Just do your best, Rick. Remember, I'll be gone part of next week and all of week after next."

"Right. I've got it written down."

The next morning, at ten fifteen, Rick called Monty and said, "Monty, I talked to Bob Dolby, the owner of Deep South Cargo Haulers, the owner of the C-130 that we've been talking about, and he said he just can't come down to five million on the C-130. He said he would take six and a half. That should make it a lot better for you, doesn't it Monty?"

"It helps, but that's still pretty high. Tell him I'll give him six, and that's as high as I will go. Are you talking to the owner or are you going through another dealer?"

"Another dealer listed it, but since you made an offer on it, they let me talk straight to the owner."

Rick, tell him that I'm not going to bargain anymore. If he doesn't want the six million, I'm going to take the older plane for two point seven. Also, did you say anything to him about pilots and loadmasters?"

"No sir. I forgot about that."

"Well, don't forget it when you talk to him again because that's a very important part of this deal. I don't have anybody qualified to fly that big a plane."

In about an hour, Rick called back. "Monty, I've got great news. Bob said he will take your offer of six million dollars, plus he has three pilots and a loadmaster that he will loan you if you're interested."

"Fantastic. You're a good man, Rick. Question. Why three pilots?"

"I asked him the same question, and he said the extra pilot was just for insurance, in case one of the other pilots got sick or something."

It was Thursday, and after several phone calls

between Rick and Bob, Bob and Monty, and Rick and Monty, it was decided that Bob and his pilots would deliver the plane to Monty at Lovel Field on Monday.

Jimmy and Monty were both excited about getting the new, old airplane, and that seemed to be all they could talk about the whole weekend. Finally, Monday rolled around and Rick called Monty at nine o'clock. "Monty, I just got a call from Bob Dolby, and they're leaving Fort Myers right now, and they should be at Lovell field in about two hours. Can you be there when they land?"

"Yeah, Jimmy and I'll be there at eleven o'clock."

"Good. I'll see you there. I'll be there, too."

Jimmy and Monty had bought the plane, sight unseen, and they were both expecting to see an olive drab or dull gray, military looking airplane land, and they were thrilled when it came into view. It was white, and not at all ugly, like they were expecting. Jimmy was already planning to have the Shepherd name and logo painted on it, when time permitted.

As soon as the pilot parked the plane in its designated place, the steps were lowered and the loadmaster exited, along with Bob Dolby. The pilots were busy working to turn everything off that was to be turned off, and before they finished the job, Monty and Jimmy wanted to board. Bob and Monty and Jimmy introduced themselves, and Bob led them up the steps to the inside of the huge airplane. When they got inside, all they could say was WOW. Jimmy said he thought there was room enough for him to go out and catch a football pass, and Monty agreed. After a brief visit inside, they deplaned and went to a place inside the terminal where they could finalize the sale. The two pilots soon joined them, and as soon as they finished their business, Monty took them to lunch.

While at lunch, Monty brought up the subject of hiring pilots and a loadmaster. I know what pilots do, but I'm not sure what Loadmasters do."

Bob Dolby pointed to Ed and said, "There's your man. He can tell you."

Ed began by saying, "A Loadmaster is basically sure that the center of gravity is in the right place when the plane is loaded. The C-130 is a giant, but if it's loaded wrong, it can become a fragile lady. For instance, let's say the plane is loaded tight on the right side with heavy equipment; bulldozers and things like that, and on the left side, it's packed tight with boxes of Styrofoam cups. It doesn't take a genius to know the plane is not loaded correctly. If you get a guy driving a forklift, and he's only interested in getting the cargo loaded and not paying attention to where he's putting things, you're asking for a potential disaster. The plane might be able to takeoff, but if the cargo weight is not placed correctly, it will be hard to fly because the center of gravity is off, and it can lead to a possible crash. In a nutshell, that's what a Loadmaster does."

You make it sound so simple, but I know it's not. Thanks, Ed.

When they finished lunch and returned to the

airport, Monty said, "Bob, can I talk to you a minute?"

They moved away from the others and he said, "Bob, I've got to have some pilots for this bird. Rick said something about you might loan me these guys. Is that right?"

"Yeah. Now that I've sold you my C-130, I don't need them anymore, unless they get trained on another plane, and I really don't need a Loadmaster because we're going to concentrate on light to medium loads from now on. If you want to hire them, and if they want to come to work for you, you have my blessings."

"Do you mind losing all three pilots plus the Loadmaster?"

"No, if you want them and they want you. I don't know how they will feel about leaving Florida. You'll have to talk to them."

"I'll tell you what. Let me just borrow them for the first trip or two, and that will give us a chance to get used to each other. While they're on loan, I'll talk to them about coming with me."

"When will your first trip be?"

"Right now, it looks as though it will be three weeks from now. We're taking over another company in San Sorento, and I have to go down there to get everything signed next week. When I get back from San Sorento, I have to go to New York the next week, and then, when I get back from New York, we'll be ready to start shipping cargo. Bob, we will be shipping mostly fabric and other things to make clothing. Will it take more than a day to load the plane? On the first trip, we'll be sending a forklift truck along with the other stuff."

"It all depends. Are your fabric rolls on pallets?"

"We're going to put them on pallets."

"How about thread and small stuff?"

"We want everything on pallets that we can get on them, but I'm sure there will be a good bit of stuff that will be loose."

"Monty, for the first time, until your people learn how to pack stuff, it may take more that one day, but after that, if your shipping department is at all efficient, I think a day will be plenty."

"That's good to know. Thanks, Bob. Let's do this. Why don't you send your guys in here on Sunday, two weeks from this Sunday, and they can make the first flight to San Sorento a day or two after that. Jimmy and I will probably go down that week, also.

Bob and his guy's plane was scheduled to leave for Fort Myers at four thirty, so Monty and Jimmy spent a little more time with them, and then they left to go back to their office.

On the way back, Monty told Jimmy, "Son, in the morning, I want to meet with everybody to see how many volunteers we're going to have to go to San Sorento. Tomorrow is payday, so just about everybody will be there. When we get back to the plant, have Sam fix some kind of a platform in the main sewing room, that we can stand on. It doesn't have to be elaborate; just something to stand on long enough for me to talk to the people."

"Okay, Dad. Listen, when do you think you and I will get to fly on our new plane? I'm anxious to try it out. I'll bet it will seem slow after flying in the G5 and 767, don't you?"

"Yeah, it'll seem slow, but three hundred and seventy-five miles an hour is still fast when you think about it."

The next morning at eight o'clock, Jimmy told Peggy, the receptionist, to get on the intercom and announce to every plant except the sock plant, that there will be a meeting of all personnel in the sewing room at plant one at nine o'clock. This will be a required meeting, and please don't be late.

About a quarter to, people began trickling in, and the stream got heavier until everybody was crowded into the sewing room at nine o'clock. The sewing room was quite large, but there were so many people in it that they were shoulder to shoulder. Most of the sewing machine operators stayed at their machines because there was actually more room there.

About five after, Jimmy began the meeting. Sam had hooked up a microphone so everybody could hear. Jimmy said, "Good morning, folks. I'm sure you're wondering why we would call a meeting on Friday morning. We have something very important to tell you, and rather than me telling you what it's about, my father is going to tell you, so here he is, Monty Shepherd." He handed the mike to Monty and said, "Okay Dad. It's all yours."

Monty took the mike and said, "It has been a while since I stood before you, but in this particular circumstance, I wanted to talk to you, myself, since I'm the one that started what I'm about to tell you rolling. How many of you have ever heard of San Sorento?"

Not one hand was raised, and Monty continued. "Recently, Joan, my wife was going through some travel brochures, and she came to one on San Sorento that advertised itself as a tropical paradise. She investigated and investigated, and to make a long story short, we called some friends of our, and the four of us went to San Sorento on vacation, and when we got there, we could easily see why they called themselves a tropical paradise because in every sense of the word, that's what it was. We checked in a nice hotel, and on the second day, there was a knock on our door.

"When we answered the door, there was a nice-looking gentleman wanting to know if I was Mr. Shepherd, and when I told him I was, he said he wanted to talk to me about a business proposition. If there was anything I did not want was a business proposition, but he said, Mr. Shepherd, if you will just give me ten minutes, I might can change your mind, and if I can't, you'll never see me again. I agreed to give him ten minutes, and as they said in The Godfather, he made me an offer I couldn't refuse. To make a long story short, we're going to go to San

Sorento and take over a company that has been manufacturing clothing, similar to what we make for over twenty years.

"Now here's why we called this meeting this morning. Most of the current and past employees of the San Sorento company are experienced, but they don't know how we want things done the Shepherd way, so we're hoping that several of you will want to go over there to help train and retrain those employees, and we hope we can make it worth your while to do that. Only those of you who are making production or piece work need to apply.

"Here's what we would like to do. First of all, we have made arrangements with a fantastic beachfront resort to rent sixty, knock your socks off efficiency apartments. If you decide you want to go, you will have your own apartment, and you won't have to share with somebody else. We anticipate that it might take six months to do the training. You will make double what you're making here. For example, if you're making eleven dollars an hour here, we'll pay you twenty-two dollars an hour over there. We'll give you a more than fair per diem and will make life as pleasant as possible while you're there, and when you're not working, you're perfectly welcome to go down to the beach.

"Elizabeth Farmer will be up here, next to the podium to get your names and other info that she needs. I failed to mention that we will need men as well. We'll need to have people experienced in laying cloth and cutting. People experienced in shipping and receiving, and maybe a fixer or two. We can't afford for too many of you to go because we still have to work here, but we think we can get by if as many as sixty of you go, Now, as I said, Elizabeth will be up front here, so feel free to come sign up. Thank you so much."

Jimmy and Monty stepped down off the platform where they had spoken and went over and stood by Elizabeth to congratulate the gang as they volunteered. About four or five minutes went by, and there was not one volunteer. Monty said to Jimmy, "Do you think we've made a mistake?"

Chapter Five

Jimmy said, "I don't think so. You've got to remember that this is something completely strange and off the wall for these people. When they've had time to think about it, I think we'll have several."

Then, in a couple more minutes, three women came to sign up, and in another minute or two, two more came. In a minute, two ladies came up to Monty and asked, "Mr. Shepherd, can we take our children? We're both single mothers, and we'd like to go, but we have children."

Monty asked, "How old are your children?" One said her little girl was ten and the other said her little boy was only four, and Monty said, "I'm really sorry, ladies, but we don't have any provisions for young children. I wish they could go, but we just don't have any way for them to be cared for."

He and Jimmy hung around for a while longer, and several more came, including two men.

Jimmy said, "Let's give it the weekend, and time for everybody to think about it, and I'll bet you that on Monday, we'll have a gang ready to go."

"I sure hope so."

Just as soon as they said that, two women came up to them and asked if the people in San Sorento spoke Spanish, and Monty said, Yes."

The one who appeared to be the spokesman for the

two said, "I'm Sofia Perez and this is my friend Champak Sandoval. We are both bottom hemmers for you, and we were wondering if we could go to San Sorento and act as interpreters as well as trainers."

Monty asked, "Are you both Mexican?"

Sofia said, "Yes sir."

Monty said, "I feel sure we can use you. Give your names to Elizabeth and be sure to tell her you speak Spanish."

After lunch, Monty thought he should call Jose to confirm that Shepherd Apparel is going to take over the San Sorento factory because there were still some unanswered questions when he and Bruno were in Chattanooga. When he called Jose's number, Jose answered immediately, "This is Jose."

"Jose, Monty Shepherd."

"Hi Monty. What's up?"

"I just wanted to call and tell you that everything is a go for the San Sorento thing. All that's left to do is for Jimmy and me to go out there for the president's and Legislature Chief's signature on the lease, and we plan to do that Tuesday. Are you still planning to go to New York?"

"Yes, definitely. I called my largest account and told them I might be getting the Shepherd line, and they promised to come see me at the show. Monty, this account has eighteen large stores and probably outsells anybody else in Mexico. They are what you call heavy hitters. Is your offer to let us catch a ride with you from Chattanooga to New York still good?"

"Absolutely. We'll leave here about eight thirty or nine o'clock Sunday morning and get to New York in plenty of time to set up the showroom Sunday afternoon. There will be Jimmy and me, our designer and three or four sales reps, plus Bryce Coleman and Jeff Ellis, and of course, you and Bruno. Everybody pitches in and helps with the set up, and if you and Bruno want to help, your help will certainly be welcome."

Jose said, "We'll be happy to help. The more we're exposed to the line, the more we learn."

"Do you have hotel reservations yet?"

"Not yet. We had to find out if we were going to represent your company first."

Monty gave him the name of his hotel and asked if he would like for him to try to get them a room, and Jose said he would.

"Jose, I've got another call coming in, so I'm going to let you go. I'll look forward to seeing you next Sunday. You'll get here Saturday night, won't you?"

"Yes. We'll get to Chattanooga on Saturday night. See ya, Monty."

Next, Monty called Bimo. When he reached him, he said, "Bimo, we have everything pretty well lined out now for us to start working at San Sorento. Jimmy and I will be there next Tuesday to get President Putra and the Legislature Chief to sign our lease. Will you please get us an appointment with both of them? It will be good if you can get both of them in the same place for the signing, so we won't have to go all over San Sorento to get it done. Also, will you get us a reservation for two single rooms at the hotel where we stay for Tuesday night only?"

"I'll take care of it for you, Monty. Call me before you get here and I'll meet you at the airport."

"Will do, and oh, Bimo, if you have any problem with the appointments, call me because I don't want to come all the way over there unless we can get everything done."

After he hung up from Bimo, he went into Jimmy's office and said, "I guess everything is on go with San Sorento except getting the signatures on the lease, and hopefully, we'll have them Tuesday. I've been thinking about taking those two Mexican girls with us to act as interpreters, but I don't guess we'll need them until later do you?"

"Not unless you're planning to talk to somebody other than Bimo and President Putra."

"I don't plan to, and I guess we can still use Bimo as interpreter the way we have been doing."

Jimmy asked, "What are we going to fly, Tuesday?

"I guess the G5, since there are only going to be the two of us," Monty said.

"That makes sense, but I'm going to miss the comfort of the 767, and I'll bet you will, too."

"You're probably right."

The weekend just flew by, and it was already time

to go back to San Sorento. Not only were they going to have to go back Tuesday, they were going to have to go to New York four days after they got back and spend almost a week, and then go back to San Sorento three days after they get back from New York. The trip after New York will more than likely take nearly a week and possibly more, so they might just take their wives.

The trip, Tuesday, went smoothly. Bimo had done everything Monty had asked him to do. The president and Legislative chief eagerly signed the lease, and they took off at eight o'clock Wednesday morning on their way back to Chattanooga.

Most of the rest of the week was spent getting ready for the New York Market. All at once the week was over and on Sunday morning, they left for the show. Just as soon as they got checked into their rooms, they left for the Mart to begin setting up the show space, and when they finished that evening, Monty treated everybody to dinner.

The next morning, when Jimmy and Monty got to the Mart, a little after eight, there was literally a line at their front door. The line was made up of both customers and sales reps waiting to kick off the market. Jimmy unlocked the door, and it was like a stampede of people rushing in to get to where they wanted to go. In some cases, the customer and rep matched up and began working. In other cases, the customer's rep had not come in yet, so they just wandered around the show room 'window shopping' until their rep got there. Show hours were officially from eight thirty to five, and there were always some that came early and stayed late.

Jose and Bruno arrived at eight twenty and used the early ten minutes to meet some of the other reps. About eight thirty, they went to the back at Jimmy's office and had a cup of coffee. While they were still drinking their coffee, Joyce Blevins, the hostess came back and asked, "Are you Jose Martinez?"

Jose said that he was, and she handed him a business card. He looked at it and said to Jimmy, "These are buyers from my largest account in Mexico City, El Palacio de Hierra. This is the account I was telling your dad about. They have eighteen large stores, and as I told your dad, they are what you say, heavy hitters. Would you like to meet them?"

Jimmy said, "Yes. I absolutely would. Do they speak English?" and Jose said they did, so he walked with him up front to meet them. When they got up to them, Jose said, "Good morning. Kelo and Tomas, I'd like for you to meet the president of Shepherd Apparel, Mr. Jimmy Shepherd. Jimmy, this pretty lady is Kelo Budi. Kelo is the ladies' buyer at El Palacio de Hierra in Mexico City, and this handsome young man is Tomas Matsos. Tomas is the men's buyer for El Palacio."

Jimmy shook hands with both of them and said, "It's a real pleasure to meet both of you. I guess Jose told you that he and his agency are now representing us in Mexico, and if there is ever anything that we can do for you, I hope you'll let us know."

Kelo said, "Thank you so much, Mr. Shepherd," and Jimmy said, "Please call me Jimmy."

Kelo said, "Okay, Jose, show me this beautiful line that you were so excited about."

Jimmy said, "Jose, while you're working with Kelo, would you like for me to show Tomas the Shepherd Staff line?"

"That would be wonderful, Jimmy. Thank you."

They went off in different directions, and it wasn't long before both Jose and Jimmy were writing. Monty saw them, but didn't want to interrupt, so he told Joyce to keep her eyes on them, and when she saw that they were finished, to call him because he wanted to meet them.

Three hours later, she saw that they were through, so she hunted and found Monty and told him she thought they were through, and he walked over to where, by that time, all four of them were standing together. Jimmy saw him first, and he said, "Kelo, Tomas, this is my father, Monty Shepherd," and Monty said, "Hi Kelo, Tomas, it's very nice to meet you. Thanks for coming in. We're very excited to have Jose representing us now, and I hope you liked what you saw."

Kelo said, "We did. You have a very nice line, and I bought a few pieces. I think Tomas gave your son an order for some men's things as well. We're excited to get it in our stores."

"Thank you, Kelo. Listen, I was just thinking

about going downstairs to grab a sandwich. I'd be happy to buy you some lunch, if you'd like to go with me."

Tomas said, "That would be great. We skipped breakfast in order to get here early. Thank you. When they got downstairs, there was a crowd, already, and only two empty tables. Jimmy told his dad what he wanted, and he sat down at one of the empty tables so they could all sit down when they got their orders.

In a few minutes they all came with their food and sat down. After they got organized, they began to talk about the market, Shepherd Apparel, Jose, and San Sorento. It seems that their store or stores were the first ones in Mexico City to buy from the new San Sorento Clothing Company, and Jose was there from the start. They told Monty and Jimmy that they hoped their relationship with Shepherd Apparel would be just as long.

When they finished their lunch, Tomas said, "Kelo we should go. Remember, we have an appointment at one thirty."

They all stood up and told each other how good it was to meet the other, and Jimmy, Jose, and Monty all three thanked Kelo and Tomas for coming by the showroom and thanked them for their order.

When Jose, Jimmy, and Monty got back upstairs, Monty wanted to see the orders they placed. They had a girl there whose sole purpose was to reconcile and total orders. She wasn't quite finished when Monty asked to see the El Palacio orders, but she promised to call him just as soon as she finished with them.

In about fifteen minutes, she tracked Monty down and showed him the totals. Kelo had placed orders for ladies' goods totaling one hundred and eighty-seven thousand dollars, American, and Tomas bought one hundred and thirty six thousand dollars for his men's orders, totaling three hundred and twenty three thousand dollars. She found Jimmy and told him that he and Jose had written that much and Jimmy said, "Not bad for a first order, hunh?"

Monty said, "Not bad at all."

That was the beginning of a very good New York show. Not only did Jose write some business but Bruno had two large accounts come in; one from Panama City, Panama, and one from Merida, Yucatan. They, like many of the large stores, only shop at the market and make notes and then wait to write the orders after they get back to their offices.

All in all, it was a very good market, and as happens at nearly all markets, it's virtually over on Thursday afternoon, and everybody is ready to go home, but the lease says that companies have to stay open through noon on Friday, so that's what they all do. In the case of Shepherd Apparel, they stayed open the full time, but some things, such as brochures and other things that had nothing to do with the sales merchandise, they were allowed to start gathering up. They fudged a little and started tearing down about ten o'clock Friday morning, and by the end of the day, the merchandise was all in boxes, ready to be picked up and taken back to Chattanooga.

Once again, everybody who had flown with the Shepherd 767 plus two or three other sales reps, who stayed over, were treated to dinner by Monty and Jimmy. It was a grand time, and all the sales reps were looking forward to getting back on the road with their fabulous new line.

Since it had been such a good market, Jimmy wanted to reward everybody by letting them sleep a little later on Saturday morning, and they didn't have to be at the airport for takeoff until ten o'clock for their three-hour flight.

When they got to Chattanooga, after saying their goodbyes, everybody went their own way, except Jose and Bruno, whose plane was already at the airport. Monty asked Jose, "Are you going back to Mexico City today, or are you going to wait until tomorrow?"

"We're going back now. You have a saying in your country that says 'strike while the iron is hot.' Well, my iron is hot, and I want to have a day's rest before I have to go on the road Monday and strike while my iron is hot."

On Monday morning, Jimmy conducted the staff meeting as he normally did, and afterwards, he went into Monty's office and they began to plan the move to San Sorento. First, they decided which styles they were going to make over there, and how many of each to begin with. Then, they gave those figures to the engineering department, so they could figure how much fabric, trim, and other things they would have to send in order to make those styles in the quantities Jimmy asked for.

They didn't realize how hard it would be to take everything they would need until they began to plan. Monty asked, "Don't we have an extra van that we're not using?"

"I think so," Jimmy said.

"Well, let's take it on this first trip, along with the forklift. I can already see that we're going to have to send the C-130 on two and maybe three trips just as fast as we can send it until we have everything we need to start production. I was hoping we could send a plane load next Monday and maybe start sewing by Wednesday, but now, I think it will be week after next before we can start sewing.

"If we send a load of fabric next Monday, it will be Tuesday before the plane is unloaded completely, and then, by the time the guys get organized enough to start spreading cloth and cutting, and the bundlers get enough bundled for the sewing room to begin sewing, it will be at least Thursday afternoon or Friday. Let me call Bimo."

When Bimo answered the phone, Monty said, "Hi Bimo. We're getting things together to send over there, and I need to know how many spreaders and cutters you've been able to hire."

"We have two spreaders and one cutter."

"Do you have anybody that knows how to bundle?"

"Yes, we have one and possibly two."

"Okay. Now, you said you have one pickup and one box truck. Is that right. You don't have any other vehicles?"

"Only the van that I have been driving. Are you going to take that away from me?"

"We might have to get you a car and take the van, so we can carry people from the Dunes to Shepherds."

"Where did you say?"

"I said Shepherds. That's the name of it now. Understand?"

"I knew that. I guess it just surprised me to hear it said out loud."

"Okay. Bimo, here's where we are right now. We plan to send a plane load of fabric and other things to you, along with another cutter and spreader, next Monday. We'll send orders of what to cut and the dozens, and the cutter we're sending will understand how to read the order. You won't be able to start sewing until week after next, and we're sending two Spanish speaking ladies to help you get started. Is your sewing supervisor somebody that we want to keep in that position?

"Yes sir. I believe you will want to keep her. She was excellent, working for us."

"Do you think she will take directions from our people?"

"I'm sure she will. If she doesn't work out to please you, I have somebody else in mind."

"Good. We'll try her to get started. Watch your people, Bimo and be sure they follow the directions from our people. We're investing a lot of money in this thing, and we want to be sure things are done right.

"In the meantime, we'll have another plane full of stuff and maybe two plane loads right behind the plane that will get there Monday. Tell your cutter to listen to the cutter we're sending, and tell your spreader to pay attention to the one we're sending because these people know what we want and how we want things, and it's important that your people know that, and oh yeah, Bimo, when the plane gets there Monday, take the people that we send to check in the Dunes as soon as they get there, and tell Pablo that this is just the beginning. More will be there in the coming days. Until we get additional transportation, you're going to have to act as a taxi and take them to the grocery store and other places they need to go. We're sending another van on the plane on Monday, so you won't have to play taxi driver by yourself very long. I think if you will show them where things are, that they can do for themselves after that. Is there anything you need to ask me?"

"Not right now. I'll call you if I need you. Bye, Monty."

When he hung up, he walked to his door and told Elizabeth to please call Sofia Perez and Champak Sandoval to come to the office. She immediately picked up a microphone and made the announcement. In about three or four minutes, they both came to the office and Elizabeth told them that Monty wanted to see them, and she led them into his office.

He said, "Hi ladies. How are you both?"

Sofia said, "We're fine, sir."

Monty said, "Are you still wanting to go to San Sorento?"

They both smiled and said, "Yes sir."

"Well, can you be ready to leave next Tuesday?"

They looked at each other and said, "Yes sir, we can be ready."

"Okay. At this point, I don't know what time. We have just bought a huge, new, old airplane to haul our fabric and stuff, and they'll be loading it next Monday. I hope they'll be finished loading it Monday. If they don't finish, it'll be Tuesday, and that might put the trip back 'til Wednesday, but I'm counting on being ready to leave Tuesday morning. One cutter and one cloth spreader will also be going at the same time, so there will be the four of you. We have a lot of apartments reserved at a resort for you to stay in, so since you're the first ones there, you'll have your choice of apartments. Since you're friends, you'll probably want to get next door to each other. Any questions?"

Sofia asked, "Did you say we'd be gone for six months?"

"We're thinking it will take about that long to get everything running the way it should. It could be a little less or it could be a little more. Will it matter to you?"

"No sir, it won't matter. Will we be able to come home some time to see our families?"

"Possibly. Our plane will be flying out and back at least once a week, and sometime, if you're at a point where you can, you might be able to catch a ride on the plane and come home for a day or two."

On Sunday afternoon, Jimmy got a phone call from Ed Harris, the Loadmaster they had talked to. He said, "Mr. Shepherd, this is Ed Harris, Loadmaster. I'm here in Chattanooga with three C-130 pilots, and we're ready to go to San Something. I can't remember the name."

"It's San Sorento. I'm glad you're here. We've got a lot of stuff ready to load, and I'll have somebody pick you up at eight o'clock in the morning. Where are you staying?"

"At the Days Inn at exit one on I-75."

"Okay, Ed. I'll see you in the morning."

The next morning, Jimmy had a van at the Days Inn promptly at eight o'clock, and the four guys were picked up and taken to the shipping department at Shepherd Apparel. As soon as they got there, Eddy Sheridan, the shipping manager came out to meet them and introduced himself to each of them. He took them inside and showed them what had been done, so far.

They were happy to see, when they got there, that much of the fabric was on pallets with the weight of each pallet taped to it. There were boxes of thread and other things on pallets, with the weights of the pallets taped on them. A Dodge van, loaded with various odds and ends was parked outside, and a forklift was just inside the door on a trailer.

Ed Harris, the Loadmaster, told Eddy Sheridan, the Shipping Manager, "Eddy, you guys have done a great job, so far. Do you know how much weight you have here?"

"I don't have any idea. I was just told to start getting this stuff together, and that we would probably have two or three loads to go, so we 've just concentrated on getting all this together and weighing it pallet by pallet. It shouldn't take much to figure it out."

Ed Harris asked, "How are we going to get it to the airport?"

"We've got a fifty-three-foot tractor trailer that we'll take it on."

"Is it ready to load?"

"As soon as you give the word."

"Okay, let's get started. Do you know the weights of the Dodge van and the forklift?"

"No, but I can get it if you need it."

"I'm going to need it, so if you will, see if you can get it."

He sent a guy out to a back lot where several trucks and cars and things like that were parked, and in just a few minutes, a pretty Kenworth Tractor and a large fifty-three-foot trailer with the Shepherd Logo painted on it drove up and backed into the loading dock.

Ed Harris asked, "Do you have something to pull the forklift with?"

"Yeah, I can use my pickup."

"Great, because we'll put the van on the plane first and the forklift last, but I'll need the weight."

"Oh. I guess I didn't think you would need it this quick. I'll get it right now," and he disappeared into the building and into his office. In about ten minutes, he reappeared and gave the figures to Ed Harris.

Next, Ed Harris asked, "Did the folks going on the flight bring their luggage this morning?"

"Yeah, it's right over there."

It didn't take long to load the trailer with two forklifts going as fast as they could run, and soon, it was full and ready to go to the airport.

Ed Harris said, "This might be all we can get on the plane. We'll have to see. I didn't realize a fifty-three-foot trailer held so much. Eddy, I'll want to load the van first, and the forklift last. Is the forklift ready to run?"

"Yeah. All you have to do is start it."

"Good, because we'll want to use it when we get to San Sorento to unload the plane and load the truck. Mr. Shepherd said there is one there, now, and that's a good thing. If my calculations are right, we should have the plane loaded before the day is over; maybe three o'clock. Do you need to call Jimmy or Monty and tell them that? I think they were planning on this load going tomorrow, but it might be early enough to go this afternoon."

Eddy called Jimmy. "Jimmy, this is Eddy Sheridan. How ya doing? Listen, Ed Harris wanted me to call you and tell you the plane may be loaded by three o'clock this afternoon, and he is wondering if you want to send it today or in the morning."

"Eddy, we've got things pretty much planned for the load to get there tomorrow, so there won't be any advantage to sending it this afternoon. We thought it would probably take all day, today, to get everything loaded, and that's why we planned it tomorrow. Dad and I will probably go out to the airport and see what the loaded plane looks like."

In about thirty minutes, Jimmy and Monty arrived at the airport and drove right up to the huge airplane. The rear ramp was still open, and they walked up it into the loaded plane. "Indescribable," Monty said. "Can you believe this thing can get off the ground and fly?"

They stayed for a little while, and then they went back to their offices. When they got there, Jimmy called down to the shipping department and told Ed Harris to get in touch with the pilots and tell them that he wanted them to take off at seven thirty the next morning. He told him to come to his office, and he would give him an envelope with instructions on what to do when they got to San Sorento.

He then called the two women and two men, that were going to go on the first flight, and told them about the seven thirty take off the next morning. He told them to be at a certain place at seven o'clock, and they would be escorted to the plane. He told them to bring a snack if they wanted one, and they should be in San Sorento by lunchtime, and they would be taken to lunch when they got there.

Finally, he called Bimo and told him that everything was loaded and ready for the first step in Shepherd Apparel taking over the San Sorento operation. He told him once again to take them to the Dunes and check them in and tell Pablo that that is just the beginning. People will be coming in a steady stream until their total is reached. He also told him to take them to lunch before they went back to the airport and began unloading the plane and taking everything to the warehouse.

He said, "Bimo, I think Dad told you that we won't begin sewing until next week because we have to have time to get cloth cut. One cutter and one spreader will be on the plane tomorrow, and they have instructions on what to do to get started. I don't know if they'll be able to begin spreading tomorrow. It'll depend on what time they get everything unloaded and over to the warehouse. It might be Wednesday before they can start. Regardless of when our guys start, have your cutter and spreader come in Wednesday morning, and they will be shown what to do. Any questions? Oh, Bimo, Dad and I will probably be there Sunday night, so we can be there when you start sewing Monday morning."

"Okay, Jimmy. I was hoping you would be here for the beginning. Would you like for me to invite the president and legislature chief also?"

"That's a good idea, Bimo. Go ahead and invite them. Dad or I will call you later this week and let you know how many people to have come to work next Monday. Are you excited?"

"Yes, I am. I'm like a child waiting on Christmas to get here."

"One last thing, Bimo. Do you know anywhere over there where you can rent or borrow another truck? If you do, it would be helpful if we had one to help unload the plane and take stuff to the warehouse."

"I'll see if I can find one."

"Okay. See ya, Bimo."

The big plane took off the next morning at exactly seven thirty. The two women were scared to death before they left because neither one had ever flown before, and they were certain that something that big could not possibly stay in the air, but after they had been in the air a few minutes, they settled down and actually enjoyed the flight.

Chapter Six

Bimo was at the airport to meet the plane when it landed, and he followed Jimmy's instructions to the letter. He took the two women and two men to the Dunes, where they checked in, and he saw Pablo and told him what Jimmy had said; that this was only the beginning.

Sofia and Champak selected rooms next to each other in a place where they thought had the best view of everything. Bill Glasser, the cutter, and Patrick Haynes the spreader, also selected rooms next to each other. While they were there, Bimo went ahead and checked Kevin, Jim and Charles, the pilots in as well as Ed Harris, the loadmaster. All they would have to do later that afternoon, when they finished unloading the plane, would be to stop by the office and pick up their keys.

From the Dunes, he took them to lunch, and it was easy to see that he liked the looks of Sofia because he directed a lot of his conversation toward her. She and Champak didn't have to go back to the airport, so Bimo took them back to the Dunes, where they took full advantage of the beautiful, sunny afternoon to enjoy the beach.

Bill and Patrick went back to the airport with Bimo because they knew what they had to spread and cut the next morning, and they wanted to be sure the cloth they would need was unloaded last, so it would be the first to get to when they needed it.

The pilots and loadmaster wanted to stay with the plane until it was unloaded, and since they didn't have lunch with the others, Bimo took them to a fast-food place for some tacos because it was quick.

He had managed to find a truck to borrow to help unload and load everything, but it still took longer to unload than it did to load in Chattanooga. Finally, around five thirty, San Sorento time, they finished up. That was seven thirty, Chattanooga time, so it had been a long day for all of them except Bimo, and he asked them what they wanted for dinner. Nobody knew what kind of food they had over there, so they left it up to him to try to please everybody. Since San Sorento was almost like a Mexican place, Sofia and Champak knew what everything was, and they tried to help the others.

After dinner, Bimo dropped everybody off at the Dunes, except Bill, and he took Bill by the warehouse to pick up the van they had left there. Everyone thought Bill was the best at directions, so that's why they chose him. He paid close attention to how they went from the warehouse to the Dunes, hoping he would be able to find the plant the next morning. As it happened, the next morning, Bimo went to the Dunes to get everybody, and after he dropped Bill and Patrick and the girls off at the plant, he took the pilots and loadmaster to the airport, so they could fly back to Chattanooga for another load.

As it sometimes happens, when something new is started, it takes a while to get everything organized and ready to actually begin the work, and that was the case with Bill and Patrick and the veterans that Bimo already had, but after a little while, they got things smoothed out and Patrick and the other spreader began spreading cloth. It was good that Sofia and Champak had come with them because without their help interpreting for Bill and Patrick, it would have been hard.

The cutting knives and spreaders were all relatively new and in very good condition, and Patrick was able to spread a cutting order in a very short time. As soon as he finished, he went to another table and began spreading another order while Bill marked patterns and cut what Patrick had spread.

Bill noticed right away that they had failed to bring a bundler with them, and he told Bimo that he needed to call Jimmy and have a bundler, or maybe two sent down on the plane the next day. Tickets and bundle cords had been sent on the first flight, so Bill thought he might be able to enlist Sofia and Champak to learn to bundle until a bundler got there, otherwise, there would be a bottleneck of unbundled cut goods with nowhere to put them. Fortunately, Sofia and Champak were familiar with the styles, and they knew what went with what, so the bundler shortage was not a total disaster. The girls seemed to actually like bundling.

That afternoon, they told Bimo that they needed

to go to the grocery store because they didn't have anything to eat at their apartment, so Bimo agreed to let them off an hour early, so they could go buy groceries. He said they passed two grocery stores on the way to the Dunes, and they could stop there if they would like. Bill had the van, so they could also go to another store if they chose to, providing they could find one.

After they bought groceries, they took them to the Dunes, and Bimo invited all four of them to go eat with him. Bill and Patrick thanked him, but said they would just stay there and fix something, since they had had food now, but Sofia and Champak went with him. He knew they were on a per diem and couldn't afford a high-dollar restaurant, so he took them to a place he liked. A place where he went a lot. It was a place where the locals went, and it wasn't very expensive. They all enjoyed the food, the evening, and Bimo especially enjoyed being with Sofia. He thought she was the best-looking thing to come along in a long time. They were all tired after a hard day's work, and he took them home soon after they finished eating.

The second day, Thursday, was a continuation of the first, except they were able to start better and faster, since they had worked out most of the kinks the day before. The girls didn't have to do much interpreting because they had pretty much explained what Bill told them to tell the other guys the day before. As a result, they started bundling soon after they got to work, and by noon, they had several canvas hampers full of bundles, ready to sew.

On Friday, the plane got there at almost exactly the same time as it did on Tuesday, but that time Eddy Sheridan had ordered lunch and a snack catered for the crew and passengers, and Bimo didn't have to take them to lunch when they got there. There were only two bundlers on the plane, and he took them to the Dunes to check in, and then he took them to the plant. By that time, there was only about an hour and a half left in the shift, so they spent part of that time with Sofia, who showed them what they had been doing and what they would be doing the next day. Normally, they wouldn't have to work on Saturday, but it was necessary that Saturday in order to get plenty for the sewers to do on Monday.

About forty-five minutes to an hour before quitting time, Bimo asked if they would like to knock off early and go buy some groceries. They wanted to do that, and while they were with him, he invited them to eat with him, since that's what he did for Sofia and Champak. They accepted his invitation, and he took them to the same place he had taken the other two the night before. He ate there so often, that he had become friends with the people who worked there, and when they saw him come in two nights in a row with four different women, they started kidding him and wanted to know if he was building a harem.

He took the pilots and loadmaster to the airport the next morning and told them, "I'll see you guys next trip. Do you know when you will be back after that one?"

Kevin said, "I don't know. I do know that they're planning to send one load per week, for sure, and maybe two loads. I guess it will depend on how fast you use up what was brought before. See ya, Bimo," and they did what they had to do in the terminal, boarded the plane and took off for Chattanooga.

When they landed that afternoon, Monty had left word that he wanted to see the four of them in his office. When they got to his office, he said, "Hi Guys. How was San Sorento?"

Kevin said, "It was great," and Jim said, "Yeah, it was good. I'd like to go there on vacation, sometime. That beach is something."

Monty said, "It's nice isn't it? Listen, the reason I called you guys in is I talked to Bob Dolby, and I told him I'd like for you all to come work for us. I made sure that he knew that I wasn't trying to steal you. He told me that he was not going to be hauling heavy air cargo any longer, and if you stayed with him, that you will have to be retrained on another kind of airplane, but at this point, he doesn't know what kind that will be because he currently has all the pilots he needs for the planes that he has. He also said that he has been thinking about discontinuing air cargo, altogether, and going to trucks only, and if I wanted to offer you guys jobs, that I would have his blessings. I took a long way around to tell you I would like to give you first choice to come with us. If you don't we're going to have to try and find some pilots, but I wanted to talk to you first. Have any of you had any thoughts in the back of your minds about becoming a Shepherd pilot?"

Kevin said, "That being the case with Bob, I think I'd like to come with you", and Ed said, "I think I'd like to come with you, too, but it's so expensive to move, especially several hundred miles, I don't know if I can afford to."

Jim said, "I would like to come with you, but my wife has a good job, and we'd have to talk about it. If she thinks she can get a job up here, then I think she'd agree to move."

"What does your wife do, Jim?"

"She works with computers. I don't know exactly."

"What if I have the lady who's the head of our computer department call and talk to her. If she could get on here, do you think you'd like to try it?"

"That would be great. She hasn't been happy for a while, and she'd probably love to work here."

Charles said, "I enjoy working for you, Mr. Shepherd, but I don't want to leave Fort Myers. I guess if Bob lets me go, I'll just have to try to find something else, but I appreciate the offer."

Monty said, "Let me throw out one more thing. If you decide to come with us, we'll move you, and you won't have to bear that expense. Now, according to what you guys have told me, Kevin wants to come and Ed does except for the moving cost, and I have just taken care of that. Jim is a 'maybe', depending on his wife's job, and Charles is a no. Here's a question for you. If I come up, one pilot short, do any of you know anybody that's looking for a pilot's job. If you do, I need to hear from you now because I can't afford to have that big C-130 sitting idle for even a week."

Charles said, "Monty, it looks as if Kevin and Jim are going to join you, and as I said, I don't want to leave Fort Myers, but if it will help you, I'll be happy to stay with you until you find all the pilots you need."

"Thank you, Charles. If you should change your mind about leaving Florida, let me know. I've been thinking about trying to get four pilots plus a backup. That way, as soon as we get unloaded in San Sorento, the plane could head back and get loaded again the next day, so even if Jim and Kevin come with us, we'll still need two and maybe three pilots qualified to fly the C -130. By the way, how long does it take to train a pilot on the C-130, if he is qualified on other types of planes?"

Kevin said, "I'd say about two months, wouldn't you Jim?"

"Yeah, two, maybe three months. It shouldn't be that hard to find them if you have time to get them trained."

Monty said, "That makes me feel better. If two of you join us, maybe we can either find another two or three or get a couple trained. Now, we don't normally work on Saturday, but we're scheduled to start sewing Monday, and we need to get another plane load of goods sent out either tomorrow afternoon or Sunday. Will you guys be able to work over the weekend?"

They all said they would, and Monty thanked them. He called Shipping, and when Eddy Sheridan answered, Monty said, "Eddy, whatta ya say?"

"Not much, Boss. What's up?"

"Eddy, I hate to ask this, but we need another C-130 load by tomorrow afternoon. Can you and your people do that?"

"Normally, I'd say we can't do it, but for you, Boss, we'll do it gladly and do another one Sunday, if you need it."

"No, no. One tomorrow is all we need right now. You're a good man, Eddy Sheridan."

"How about telling that to my wife?"

"If I see her, I will, but I'm sure she knows it."

One of Eddy's men picked Ed Harris up at seven o'clock Saturday morning, and they began loading the plane. Monty was leaving it up to Ed and the pilots as to when they were going to leave, that afternoon or Sunday morning, and they decided to leave Saturday afternoon so they would have all day Sunday to just loaf around and enjoy the beach. When they told Jimmy, he and Elizabeth began calling some of the volunteers that were going. On that trip, there would be twenty six passengers, and they, too would have Sunday off, except, most of them would have to go to the grocery store, after they got there, and it would take both vans maybe two trips to handle that chore. Jimmy encouraged them to take some things with them on the plane, but not in loose grocery bags. He and Elizabeth gave each of them detailed instructions on the time and location of their meeting point.

The original loading of the C-130 took the better part of the day, and the second load took quite a bit less time, and on this upcoming load, Ed was guessing that if they started at seven thirty or eight o'clock, they would be finished by noon, and his guess was really close.

There were three or four fast food places at the airport, and Shepherd Apparel had worked out a deal with each of them to give whatever the bearer of a yellow card wanted, with a ten-dollar limit. Ed announced that the loading was complete, and if anybody wanted anything to eat, to get it right then because they would be taking off at one o'clock, and there was no food on the plane.

Some of the people went to get something to eat right then, but it looked as if most of them got 'to go' orders and took their lunch on the plane to eat after they took off. They had been told that the flight would take five hours. At one o'clock, everyone was on the plane, and Kevin started the big engines. In a minute, they were taxiing down the runway, and at the end of the runway, Kevin turned the plane around. As soon as he turned it around, he gunned the engines, released the brakes, and sprinted down the runway in the opposite direction. He gave it full throttle, increasing the speed of the giant plane until it got to a speed of three hundred and eighty five miles per hour, and then he pulled back on the wheel, and they were airborne.

Some of the folks had not flown before, and they were nervous at first, but soon settled down. Jim asked those who had brought food on board to please wait until they got to altitude before opening their bags.

It was only a few minutes until they were high enough to open their bags and eat their lunch. When they did, it was almost like break time in the Shepherd plant in Chattanooga, except there was no smoking on the plane. Everyone seemed to have taken their minds off the fact that they were twenty-seven thousand feet up in the air, going about four hundred miles an hour.

At five o'clock, San Sorento time, they touched down, and the excitement began to grow. Bimo drove one van and Bill Glasser drove the other one to meet them at the airport. By the time they got all their luggage loaded, there was only room enough for seven people in each van. Bimo asked everyone if they would like to stop and get some groceries on the way to the Dunes, but nobody wanted to. They were all anxious to get to see the beach and their apartments. That would be the first time for some of them to ever see the ocean.

When they got the first load to the Dunes, Bimo went into the office with them and helped them check in. Then, he appointed Sofia to be in charge when they brought the second load in. There was a total of twenty six trainers on the plane plus the crew of four., and when they finally got everybody checked in, Bimo held a meeting with everybody outside by the pool.

He said, "Welcome to San Sorento. I hope you're going to like it here. Now, it's after seven o'clock, your time, and you're probably hungry. Arrangements have been made for everybody to eat this evening at the Pueblo Grill, a restaurant that serves both American food as well as Mexican. It's just up the street about two blocks, and you can either ride in the van or walk, and if you want to eat there, we need to go now. I see that some of you brought food with you, and if you did and have food for breakfast, you may not want to go to the grocery store this evening, but for those of you who didn't bring anything with you, Bill and I will be taking whoever wants to go, to the store after we eat. You might just want to get enough for breakfast and maybe dinner tomorrow and then stock up on food after you get off Monday. Both vans will be available to you, and there are also cabs, if you would rather use one of them. I must warn you, though, not many cab drivers speak English.

"I hope that when Messrs. Jimmy and Monty

Shepherd get here, that they will make arrangements for some better transportation for you, but in the meantime, the vans will have to do. In the mornings, the vans will begin running at six forty-five, and hopefully, we can get everyone to the plant before eight o'clock.

"Day after tomorrow is going to be a special day for Shepherd Apparel San Sorento. It will be the first day for the company, and not only will Messrs. Jimmy and Monty be here, but the President of the country of San Sorento and the Chief of the San Sorento Legislature will be here, also. By the time each VIP says a few words, it will probably be around nine o'clock. When you get to the plant, in the mornings, please go to the break room, and you will be told what to do. Again, welcome to San Sorento. I'm looking forward to working with each one of you. Now, let's go eat. I'm hungry, and I know you are."

About six o'clock, Saturday evening, Jimmy and Monty landed at the airport in their Gulfstream Five, better known as G5. They took the limo to the Holiday Shores Hotel, where they usually stayed and had dinner in the hotel dining room almost immediately after they got there. They had thought that they would arrive earlier, so they didn't have any food catered to the airplane before they left Chattanooga. Something had come up, and they were late leaving Lovell Field, thus, making them late getting to San Sorento.

While in the dining room. Monty told Jimmy, "I'll

bet next week is going to be a circus.”

“Why do you say that?”

“Because we’re pretty much starting from scratch, and most of the people don’t know how to speak English.”

“How many of our people do you think can speak Spanish?”

“I don’t know of any, except Sofia and Champak.”

“How many of the San Sorento people speak English? Do you know?”

Monty said, “I have no idea, but I would guess there are several. Bimo will know. You know, I hope we haven’t started this thing up too fast.”

“What do you mean, Dad?”

“Well, if we had been really smart, we wouldn’t have rushed the opening as fast as we did. We would have taken the time to spread the operations out. For instance, let’s say there are eight operations that you have to do on each garment, from start to finish. It would have been so much easier if we had done the first operation today and the second operation tomorrow and so on. Instead, we’re trying to start from scratch by doing the whole thing in two or three days, and not allowing enough time between operations, to be sure the quality is there. I’m just afraid we’re going to be sorry we’ve done it this way when all is said and done.

“Also, we’re trying to open a major manufacturing plant without a plant manager or a sewing supervisor. We’re just depending on our Chattanooga volunteers to take those parts. I feel sure we can promote some good people to those positions. All I'm saying is I think we rushed the opening too much. Starting Monday is fine, but we should have spread out the other operations until they were ready to be done. Oh well, we'll just have to try and get through it. If we can make it through next week, I think the weeks after that will be smoother and more efficient."

"I see what you mean, but everybody in San Sorento is so excited, most of the operators are going to be patient enough to go along with whatever happens. If we see we're going to get into a bottleneck, we can always have some of the operators take off a day or maybe two, and I don't think they'll mind as long as they know they're going to get to come back."

"I guess you're right. We'll just have to see how Monday goes. You know something else?"

"What?"

"It seems as if we're left God completely out of most of this. We asked Him to help us and to let us know if we should open this place, and He said we should, and I've thanked Him over and over, and I'm sure you have, too, but you know what? I don't remember ever seeing a church in San Sorento. I've seen what the locals refer to as church, and I'm not sure what they worship, but I haven't seen even one Christian place of worship. Have you?"

"Now that you mention it, I don't remember seeing any."

Monty said, "Well, I think most of our people are used to going to church, and I don't intend to create a situation where they can't worship."

"What are you thinking, Dad?"

"I'm thinking that if I have to, I'm going to build them some kind of church. It may have to be redoing a home or renting space in a hotel or something. Anything where the people can go to worship."

"Do you think if you build a church and our people go home in a few months, that it will be used after they're gone?"

"I don't know, Son. Maybe if we and our people can lead a few people to Jesus while we're here, they will still use it. Boy, look at the time. I didn't realize it was this late. Why don't we go up to our rooms and get some rest? Tomorrow's going to be our last day off for a while, so we need to enjoy it."

Jimmy said, "I'm looking forward to it. I plan to spend a good part of it at the beach."

"I'll probably be out there with you," Monty said.

Sunday was a very good day. The weather was sunny and warm, with a gentle breeze just strong enough to make it comfortable and not too hot. Jimmy and Monty had a leisurely breakfast before they made their way down to the beach, spread their beach towels, laid down on them, and in just a few minutes, they were both asleep. They slept for a while, and when they woke up, Monty asked, "You want to walk up the beach? The Dunes is only a couple of blocks, so why don't we go see who's out there and what they're doing?"

"Okay. Let me get my shirt on."

They began walking up the beach, and when they got to within sight of the Dunes, the first two people they saw were Bill Glasser and Patrick Haynes. When they got closer, Bill and Patrick saw them, and they all shook hands and began talking. Bill said, "The plane just arrived a few minutes ago, and everyone seems excited. What are you guys doing here? Did you come for the opening?"

Jimmy said. "Yeah, it's supposed to be something. The president of San Sorento and celebrities on down are going to be there."

Bill said, "Yeah, I know. Bimo gave all of us instructions yesterday."

Monty asked, "Patrick, have you ever met a president?"

"No sir. This will be my first, and if I like it, I may just go on to Washington and meet the real one."

Monty said, "What are you talking about? President Putra is a real one."

"I'm sure he is, and I'm sure I'll be happy to meet him."

As they were talking, some of the Shepherd women saw them and came over to where they were.

None of the women had ever seen Jimmy or Monty dressed in anything other than business clothes that they wore to work, and most of them couldn't take their eyes off of Jimmy, and the older ones couldn't stop looking at Monty. Both had been outstanding athletes in college and Jimmy went on to play professional baseball until he got hurt and had to quit, and they both tried their best to keep in good shape, and according to the way the women looked at them, they had been successful doing it.

Before long, nearly all who were out there came to where they were, and for the next few minutes, it was just a maze of questions and answers. What do you think about this place? Do you like your apartment? Do you think you're going to like it over here? Do you think you'll be able to understand what the people say when you work with them? Are you glad you came?

Some of the questions were directed to Jimmy and Monty, such as, how did you ever find this place? Are you going to move Shepherd Apparel down here? Are you going to transfer people from Chattanooga down here? Can we ride the plane home some weekend? Can I get my son or daughter down here sometime? When are the rest of our people going to get here?

Monty attempted to answer some of their questions. The one about how did he find this place, he said, "I told you that when we had our meeting, asking for volunteers."

To the question about moving Shepherd Apparel down here, he said, "No." To the question about transferring people from Chattanooga down here, the answer is, "No, unless someone requests that we transfer them, but I can't imagine that happening. To your question about going home some weekend, the answer is, "Possibly. If your particular job is so you can, and if the plane is scheduled just right, I have no problem with you going home for a couple of days, and finally, can you bring your son or daughter down here, the answer is, I don't know. If the son or daughter is younger than sixteen or seventeen, the answer is no. We're just not set up to take care of younger children. If your child is older, and the plane schedule is such, then we might take a look at it, and finally, the rest of your group is scheduled to get here tomorrow afternoon."

They all stood around and talked for another twenty or thirty minutes, and then Jimmy and Monty broke away and walked back to their hotel's beach. Sometime, on their walk, Monty asked Jimmy, "Do we have any more vans or other vehicles in our motor pool that are not being used right now?"

"I don't know, off hand, but there probably are some."

"Do you know how to reach any of our people on the weekends?"

"Yeah, I've got all our key people on my computer in the hotel."

"Good. When we get back, how about calling Eddy Sheridan or whoever you think best to call and ask them what kind of vehicles we have that aren't being used right now. If there is a van or something else that has plenty of room, tell them to fill it up with gas and try to get it on the next plane to here. We actually need two vans or at least a van and a car. Have two sent if we have them."

Chapter Seven

Jimmy called Eddy Sheridan when they got back to the hotel and luckily, Eddy knew some of the vehicles that were parked and not being used. Among them was an older model three seat Suburban and a Ford Explorer. When he told Monty, Monty said, "Tell him to send both the Suburban and the Explorer, and to be sure they're both in running order. Check the batteries and fill them both up with gas, and if he has to leave off a few bolts of cloth in order to get them in, to do it. If he has to leave off some cloth, we can make it up on the next load, and tell him to go out there this afternoon, if he can, to make sure they will run. Tell him that I'll make it up to him when I get back."

When Jimmy called Eddy, the plane was already mostly loaded, and when he told Ed Harris what Jimmy wanted, they stopped loading the remainder immediately.

Eddy called the Chevrolet dealer and got the weight of the Suburban and the Ford dealer to get the weight of the Explorer. When he gave the weights to Ed, he didn't say anything. He just muttered something under his breath and told the forklift driver, closest to him, "You're going to have to take three pallets of fabric off the plane and back to the warehouse. They want us to bring two vehicles, and we've got to make room for them."

It didn't take long to get everything done, and they closed up the large loading ramp underneath the plane.

The next morning, they took off at seven thirty with twenty-seven more people on it. Those twenty-seven added to the first twenty six and those added to Sofia and Champak and the two bundlers totaled fifty seven from the Chattanooga plants.

At about the same time, Monday morning, everything looked as though it was going crazy with two vans taking people from the Dunes to the plant two times plus all the new employees going to work and the hotel limousine delivering Monty and Jimmy from the hotel to the plant. The President and his security team as well as the other VIPs added to it.

Pretty soon, everyone had arrived and had found a place for the opening festivities at the San Sorento plant.

Bimo acted as emcee. He made some very brief remarks and then introduced President Arin Putra, President of San Sorento who welcomed Shepherd Apparel to his country. President Putra sat down, and then Bimo introduced Guido Vasquez, the Chief of the San Sorento Legislature. After Guido's remarks, Bimo introduced Jimmy, who spoke briefly and said how happy the Shepherd Apparel Company was to be there. After Jimmy, Bimo introduced Monty, and in his introduction, he made sure the people knew how the whole thing between San Sorento and Shepherd

Apparel began. At the end of his introduction of Monty, everybody stood; even President Putra and Chief Vasquez.

Monty thanked everyone for their warm welcome and told them about his vision for the San Sorento plant. He said, "I want you to know that I believe God has led me to San Sorento because when I asked Him for His guidance, He made every step take place without complications. Two months ago, I had never heard of San Sorento, and look where we are now. I want you to understand that each of you former and current employee are going to have excellent job security as long as you do your jobs the way you are expected to. I ask for your patience as we start up from scratch. Jimmy and I have been in such a hurry to get started that it might be necessary to let some of you off for a day or two if things begin to bottleneck, but I assure you that if we do have to let you off for a day or so, it will definitely be only temporary. It will just be a matter of trying to get things smoothed out. I assure you that we have plenty of business and more coming in, and with all of your help, the Shepherd Apparel San Sorento plant is going to be a huge success." He then sat down, and once again, everybody stood and gave him a standing ovation.

Bimo went over and took the microphone and asked all the Chattanooga people to meet in the break room and for all seamstresses to go to the back of the sewing department. Then he called Maria Reyes and Sofia Perez and Champak Sandoval and anybody else that could speak English to meet in the outer office.

At the same time, while everyone was going to their designated places, Monty, Jimmy, Guido, and President Putra stood where they had been speaking and talked. The President and Guido assured them that they would do anything and everything to help them, and they thanked them profusely for coming there. Soon, they broke up, and Jimmy and Monty went to the office where Bimo and the ones who could speak English had gone.

There was a man in there who Monty hadn't seen before, and Bimo introduced him as Luiz Garza and said he had hired Luiz to be the new plant manager. He had worked at San Sorento Clothing a few years earlier as a general supervisor and assistant plant manager, but he had quit because of friction between him and the then plant manager. Bimo told Monty he hired Luiz on a three-month trial basis.

There were seven or eight women in the office that said they could speak English in addition to Sofia and Champak, and Monty thought that was great. They were already employed there and knew what they were doing with a sewing machine, and after working a little bit with the trainers, they could help train some of their peers as well.

In a little bit, Maria called all the operators over to where the close shoulder seamers worked. She asked the close shoulder seamers to take a machine, and seven or eight did just that. Then she asked the others if they knew how to close shoulders and several said they did, so she asked them to sit down and help with closing shoulders. Closing shoulders is a fast operation, and with fifteen or sixteen women doing it, it didn't take but a few minutes for several dozen tops to be ready for the next operation.

The next operation was setting sleeves, and Maria did the same thing she did with shoulders. She asked for the experienced ones first and then others who could do it, and soon there were several dozen tops ready to have the sides closed.

Same thing with the side closing, but then, when it came to bottom hemming, production slowed down. A good bottom hemmer can turn out an amazing amount of hemmed garments, but in order to do a good job hemming, one has to have quite a bit of training and experience, so the way Maria was doing with the previous operations, wouldn't work with the hemming. All in all, though, Maria was very smart to do the way she did in order to get production started, and by the end of the day, there were dozens and dozens of garments completely made except for the bottom hemming, and there were several dozens of them.

Maria asked Bimo if she could do that the next day until they got enough done to keep everybody busy with their regular jobs. She also wanted him to have the inspectors wait and come in on Wednesday, and the folders and packers the day after that. He saw how well that was working, and he said they could do it that way until they got the initial production smoothed out.

The way they had to work that first day allowed some of the Chattanooga gals to sew some and their work helped create more dozens. The workday ended and everyone was pretty tired because it had been a long, stressful day. The Chattanooga folks had to load up in the two vans and half of them made the first trip to the Dunes, and the other half had to wait for the second trip. It wasn't too bad, though, because there were only about fifteen minutes between trips.

When they got to the Dunes, it was almost like a reunion. While they were working, the other plane came in, and the other half of the trainers were there. Bimo had designated two women, who could speak broken English to meet them at the airport and take them to the Dunes, and to buy groceries if they wanted to. Several did want to, but some didn't. They had brought a few items with them, and they thought they had enough for breakfast the next morning and would go get groceries the next day. They let grocery shopping go so they could go to the beach.

After the ones who were in the first half had supper and changed for the beach, many of the ones in the second half joined up with them and wanted to know everything that had taken place up to that point. Most of those who had been at work all day shared just about everything with them, and the majority was very positive, but as in all groups, some are more negative, but even those who didn't have such a positive outlook weren't that negative.

Bimo came by later and asked the new arrivals to

come out to the pool so he could talk to them. They did, and he welcomed them the way he did the first group and told them what to expect the next morning. He told them that the vans would start running at six forty five, and he asked everybody to be ready at that time. It had taken two trips with each van to get everybody on the first group delivered, so he looked for it to take four trips now, since there are twice as many people. He pointed out that there were only about fifteen minutes between trips. He said it would work that way as long as they were there, and then after they all went back to Chattanooga, the normal hours of seven to three thirty would start.

Hustle and bustle was the thing at the Dunes, the next morning. As expected, it took both vans four trips to get everybody from the resort to the plant, and after they got there, Maria and Bimo had to decide what each person was to do. If an operator had been working at San Sorento Clothing and had been setting sleeves, for example, then she would set sleeves with the new company. With the ones who were there now, and the ones who had been hired, but hadn't started to work yet, there were approximately two hundred sewing machine operators. Jimmy had set a goal of fifteen thousand dozen garments per week, and with that number of operators, they should be able to make that. It was going to take another hundred to a hundred and fifty inspectors, folders and packagers. Those figures were based on every operator making production or piecework as it's sometimes called, but of course, seldom does everybody make that all the time. This new plant stands a pretty good chance to hit the set goal with that many experienced people in place.

About mid-morning, Monty told Jimmy, "Son, why don't you go back in the morning? I may stay here the rest of the week. I can hitch a ride on the C-130."

"Why are you going to stay? Don't you think with all these trainers and Bimo and Maria, they can handle things?"

"Yeah, I think they can handle things, but there's something I've got to do, and it may take me a few days to do it."

"What are you going to do, Dad?"

"I'm going to see about finding a place for our people to worship."

"Who are you going to get to preach?"

"I don't have any idea. We probably won't have a preacher, but maybe I can find somebody to lead some kind of a worship service. You go on home. You need to look after the business there. I want to at least try this. I don't have the schedule, but the plane should be going back to Chattanooga Friday or Saturday."

"Okay, if that's what you want to do. I'll tell the guys to be ready to take off around eight in the morning. Dad, why don't you set aside the Suburban or Explorer for us to use when we're down here? Don't you think that would be better than having to depend on Bimo to take us everywhere?"

"You're probably right. I'll think about it. Right now, why don't you go out and watch the production and see if you can think of any changes we need to make. I need to go talk to Bill Glasser for a minute. I'll meet you back here in a little bit."

He left Jimmy and made his way through the mass of sewing machines and into the cutting department. He watched a couple of guys spreading cloth for a few minutes, and then he spotted Bill Glasser cutting an order that had already been spread. He walked over to Bill and said, "Hi Bill. Can I talk to you for a second?"

"Hi Monty. Sure. What can I do for you?"

"Bill, am I right when I think that you teach Sunday School at home?"

"Yes sir. I teach a married couple's class."

"That's what I thought. Bill, when I first came to San Sorento on vacation, I wasn't interested in even hearing about this place when Bimo knocked on my hotel door and said he had a proposition he wanted to share with me. He was so insistent and told me if I would just give him ten minutes, that he would leave me alone if I didn't like what he said. He was so convincing that I took him up on his invitation to show me the plant. When I saw this place and heard what they were prepared to do for us, I thought that that was like the Godfather movie; they made me an offer I couldn't refuse. Well, long story short, Bill, I prayed about it and Jimmy prayed about it, and we both felt like it was something we were supposed to do, so we set the wheels in motion, and here we are.

"Now, here's what I wanted to talk to you about. First, before I tell you, have you seen any churches in San Sorento? I'm talking about Christian Churches."

"No sir. I can't recall seeing any."

"Well, I haven't either, and I want to do something about it. I'm not sure what the people over here worship, but I don't think its God, or else there would be some churches. Shepherd Apparel has fifty-seven people over here helping train the employees of our new plant here, and I'm sure many of them go to church at home. We're talking about keeping most of them over here for six months, and that's a long time without going to church. Now, if I can find somewhere where we can gather to worship God, would you be willing to help lead the folks attending to a Devotional or maybe a Bible study?"

"Monty, I'd be happy to do that. The only thing is, I don't have anything but my Bible and a book of devotions over here with me, and I'm pretty sure there aren't any stores here that sell Christian literature. I'll do what I can with my Bible if you want me to."

"Thank you, Bill. I haven't started looking for a place yet, so I can't tell you anything, but if you're willing like you said, I'm going to start looking tomorrow. Jimmy's going home tomorrow, and I'm going to hitch a ride on the big plane at the end of the week or the first of next week, if I can get this worship place settled. I'll let you know if and when I find a place."

"Okay, Monty. Good luck."

Monty turned around and headed back to meet Jimmy, and before he got too far, Bill hollered for him. He turned around and said, "Did you call me?"

"Yes sir, I did. I just want you to know that I appreciate you, and I appreciate working for you."

"Thanks, Bill. I really appreciate that. That means a lot to me."

He went back to the office that Bimo used, where Jimmy was waiting for him, and Bimo was there. He told him, "Bimo, I think I'm going to take the Suburban to use while I'm here, and I told Jimmy to go on home, tomorrow. I'm going to stay here a few more days, and you won't have to haul me around. Would you rather have the Explorer to use or would you rather keep the van?"

"I think I would rather have the Explorer until I have to haul a bunch of people."

"That's fine. If you have to, the van will be here, so do what you'd rather do."

"Thank you, Monty."

"Jimmy, are you hungry?"

"I'm starving."

"Me too. Let's go to the Pueblo Grill. They are supposed to serve American food as well as Mexican, so let's see if they know how to make a cheeseburger with fries."

"Sounds good to me."

They went into the restaurant and sat down. When the waitress came, she couldn't speak English, and Monty asked her if there was anybody there that could. She turned around and walked off, and in just a minute, another waitress came and said, "Hi fellas. What can I get for you?"

Surprised at her good command of English, Monty said, "Do you have hamburgers?"

She said, "Yes."

He asked, "How about cheeseburgers?" and she said, "Yes," and he asked, "How about French fries?", and she said, "Yes, we have French fries."

He said, "Good. Let us have two cheeseburgers, two French fries and two Coca Colas. Did you know that the first Coca Cola was bottled in the town where we live?"

"Where do you live?" she asked.

"Chattanooga, Tennessee, "he said."

"Oh, you must be the men who are opening the San Sorento Clothing Company."

"That's us, but the name of it now is Shepherd Apparel Company/ San Sorento. I am Monty Shepherd, and this is my son, Jimmy Shepherd."

"It's nice to meet you. Thank you for opening the clothing company again. It will help us." She told them her name, but neither one could understand what she said.

She disappeared and in a few minutes, she returned with their order, and surprisingly, it was just as close to a cheeseburger in the United States as you could get.

While they were eating their lunch, Monty said, "I feel so relieved about things now that we have the plant open that I think I'll take off this afternoon. Would you like to go to the beach?"

Jimmy said, "You know, I was just thinking the same thing. Yeah, I'd like to go to the beach. This will probably be my last time for a while."

With a big grin, he said, "I know, and your mother and I will be thinking about you while we're in Florida playing golf and eating Grouper."

"When are you going to Florida?"

"I don't know. We haven't talked about it, but we haven't been down there since before we came here the first time. I'm sure if we don't go soon, your mother will call Tracy Martin, and they'll go without me, and I don't want that to happen."

They did what they said they were going to do. When they finished lunch, they went outside and got in the Suburban and went to the hotel and changed into their swim trunks. Monty said, "You know, it feels good, being able to drive somewhere, without having to depend on somebody else to take me. I just wish I knew where I was going."

They spent the better part of the afternoon at the beach, and when it became time, they went in and got out of their trunks. They drove the Suburban to the Italian restaurant they liked so well.

While they ate, they talked about what Jimmy was going to do when he got back to his office, and he said, "I've got so much to do, I can't tell you what

I'm going to do first. I've really gotten behind, spending so much time down here. Thankfully, we've got good people that can take up the slack. When do you think we'll be able to start shipping out of here?"

Monty said, "I would say in about two weeks."

"Well, when we make our first big shipment to Jose and Bruno, I want to go to Mexico City. I've got to get to Munich sometime. We've gone into so many different countries since you opened the Munich office and warehouse, I don't want them to think we've deserted them."

"Son, what do think about promoting somebody to be an International Sales Manager to help Bryce. I think we've put too much on him. We could keep him on as manager of the Western Hemisphere and promote somebody else to be manager of the Eastern Hemisphere, or if Bryce would prefer, we could put him in the east and promote someone else for the west."

"You know, it seems like I've always heard of the Western Hemisphere, but I don't remember ever hearing about the Eastern Hemisphere. Do you know which is which?"

"I'd have to get the map, and then I'd probably make mistakes, but we live in the Western Hemisphere. I know the Eastern Hemisphere consists of Europe, Asia, Australia and others that I don't know, but I do know that Shepherd Apparel does business in both of them. What do you think about what I said?"

"I really haven't thought about that, but you're right. Bryce has too much on him, especially now that we've added Mexico and Central America. I'll get on that when I get home. I'd like to have your input on whoever we pick. Maybe we can get our heads together when you get home."

"Okay. Are you ready to go?"

"I'm ready."

They went to their hotel, and each went to his own room. Jimmy called Analisa and told her that he would be home the next day, and his dad was going to stay for a few days. Monty called Joan and told her that he was going to stay a few more days, and he explained why he was staying. He told her that Jimmy would be home the next day. Both of them were tired, so they turned in early.

Chapter Eight

The next morning, Monty took Jimmy to the airport in time for the eight o'clock takeoff, and then he returned to the hotel and had breakfast in the dining room. Jimmy was going to eat on the plane. The first place Monty wanted to go that morning was the Dunes Resort. He hoped they had some kind of conference room that they would let him use for Sunday morning services. He would rent it if he had to.

When he got to the Dunes, he went into the office, and he knew the girl there couldn't speak English, so he walked up to her and simply said, "Pablo?"

She answered, "Si. Uno momento," and she disappeared into the back. In a minute, she came back out with Pablo about two steps behind her. He said, "Monty, good morning."

Monty answered with "Good morning, Pablo. How are you doing?"

"I'm fine. What can I do for you this morning?"

"Pablo, I'm looking for a place where my people can gather on Sunday mornings and worship. Would you have such a place?"

"Yes, we have such a place, but I cannot let you use it."

"Why not?"

"Because it would be too dangerous."

"What do you mean?"

"The followers of The Church of the First Born of the Lamb of God would not permit it."

"Do they own the resort?"

"No, they do not own the resort, but if they found out we were letting some other group worship here, someone could get killed or the Dunes could even get burned down. I'm sorry, Monty, but I can't let you use our facilities for worship."

"I don't understand, Pablo. How can a group that has the name, 'Lamb of God', be so dangerous?"

"I don't know, but they are."

"Well, thank you, anyway, Pablo."

What Pablo said bothered Monty, and he didn't know exactly what to do. Was Pablo just paranoid or was there a legitimate threat by that group? He thought he would go see if Bimo knew anything about them, so he drove out to the plant to see him.

When he walked in the office, he told one of the girls to page Bimo and ask him to come to the office. He must have been busy because it took him about eight full minutes to get to the office. He looked at Monty and said, "Good morning, Monty."

Monty replied, "Good morning, Bimo. Did I catch you at a bad time?"

"No, I was just trying to make an operator understand how to make a pleat, but Maria came to my rescue. What can I do for you?"

Monty smiled and asked, "Do you know how to make a pleat?"

Kidding, Bimo said, "Man, yeah. I'm the king pleat maker."

"That's good to know. Maybe we can get you to Chattanooga, sometime."

"Just let me know when. Now, I know you didn't come here this morning to talk about pleats. What can I do for you, Monty?"

"Bimo, I'm trying to find a place where my people can go to worship on Sundays. I just came from the Dunes. I thought they might have a conference room or something like that, where we could gather. When I asked Pablo about it, he had a look of fear on his face, and he said he didn't have a place to worship. I asked why we couldn't use the conference room, and he said it was too dangerous. I questioned him some more, and I asked why was it dangerous, and he said because the Church of the First Born of the Lamb of God might kill him or some of the worshippers or they could very well burn the Dunes down. I thanked him and left. I didn't know if he was actually afraid or if he was just being paranoid."

"I can tell you that he was not being paranoid. The Church of the First Born of the Lamb of God is a vicious organization. Pablo was not kidding or exaggerating with either one of his statements. He could very well be killed if he let you use his place for worship."

"Do you know anything about this group?" Monty asked.

"As a matter of fact, I do. When they first came to

San Sorento, I was curious, and so I studied them. First of all, their full name is The Church of the First Born of the Lamb of God, and they're a violent Latter Day Saint group founded by a man named Ervil LeBaron, and they are responsible for dozens of deaths over two decades. After his death, it was run by several of his sons."

"Do you know who Joseph Smith was?"

"Yeah, he founded the Mormon Church."

"That's right. When he founded the Latter Day Saint movement, Benjamin Johnson was one of his earliest followers. Johnson followed the church teaching and practiced polygamy. When the Church of Jesus Christ of Latter Day Saints renounced polygamy, Johnson and his family, like many Mormon fundamentalists, continued the practice. In 1924, Johnson's grandson, Alma Dayer LeBaron, Sr., moved his family to Mexico where the government showed no interest in prosecuting polygamy. They settled near Colonia Juarez, Chihuahua.

"Alma Dayer believed that Johnson was the rightful successor to Smith and that Johnson had appointed him to follow him. After Alma's death, several of his sons claimed to be his true successor. In 1955, his son, Joel founded The Church of the Firstborn of the Fullness of Times and named himself as president. His brother, Ervil, became second in command, with full authority over their new settlement, known as Colonia LeBaron.

"By 1967 tensions were riding high between Joel

and Ervil. Ervil began advocating for the return of the former Mormon principle of blood atonement. This required that a sinner must have their blood shed in order for them, to have a place in heaven. Essentially, it required the death penalty for actions deemed crimes by Ervil. Joel refused to allow the practice in his church. The brothers also argued about many other things.

"By the late 1960's, Ervil LeBaron began preaching against his brother, accusing him of crimes against their faith. Proclaiming that he was the true successor to his father, Ervil began the Church of the First Born of the Lamb of God, and he named himself the president. Some of Joel's followers switched their allegiance to Ervil.

"In 1972, Ervil orchestrated the murder of his brother, the first victim of the blood atonement policy. To Ervil's surprise, Joel's followers did not flock to his side; instead they advocated for Ervil's arrest. He was convicted of planning the murder, but he was released a year later.

"Ervil remained the leader of the cult, and several of his family were victims of his blood atonement policy, and was most interested in executing his brother Verlan, who Joel's followers had elected as their new leader. Fearing for his life, Verlan went into hiding.

"Monty, I won't take up any more of your time talking about this church and this family. They went on for several more years with Ervil declaring himself as the true successor and murdering more of his family; brothers, children, and even wives. There's one more brief story I want to tell you before I quit.

"On June 27, 1988, the cult targeted three names that were prominent on Ervil LeBaron's blood atonement list. Within the span of a few minutes around four p.m., cult members killed four people in three different locations in Texas.

"I could go on for a long time about this cult, but I think you get the idea why people are afraid of them. The church is not nearly as active as it once was, but Ervil LeBaron's Church of the First Born of the Lamb of God still has followers in San Sorento and I would suggest that you not offend them You sure don't want to get on Ervil's blood atonement list. That's why Pablo didn't want you to have your religious meeting at the Dunes."

"Wow, I had no idea there were still organizations like that around. Bimo, thank you. I may have to rethink my plans."

"What do you think you'll do, Monty?"

"Right now, I'm not sure. I've got to do some praying about it. It all depends on what I think God tells me to do."

"How will you know what He wants you to do?"

"Well, there are ways, Bimo. One might be if I can't find a place to meet, He might be telling me that I shouldn't try anymore. Another might be if I find a place to meet and then when people find out about it, threats are made to me or some of my people. That might be God talking to me. One thing I know for sure, Bimo, is I'm not going to leave nearly sixty people down here without any way to worship for five or six months. If it comes to that, I'm going to take them back home where they'll be safe. Let me ask you something; Does San Sorento have a police department?

"Yeah, we have a police department."

"Do you think they are afraid of Ervil's church?"

"I really don't know, Monty. I don't know if there has ever been any other religious group come to San Sorento, so they might not even know themselves."

"I hope I don't have to, but I may have to put them to the test. Okay, Bimo, thanks for the information. I'll see you later."

"Oh, Monty, I want to tell you something. I don't know what Shepherd Apparel's policy is, but I have invited Sofia Perez to go to dinner with me tonight. Is that alright?"

"As far as I'm concerned, it is. We don't have any company policy about that. I hope you two have a good time."

"Thank you, Monty."

Monty left Bimo and thought he would go back to his hotel, and while he was there, he would ask the manager about letting his people use one of their conference rooms on Sunday mornings for a worship service. The first thing he did when he got there was to go up to his room and pray. He asked God to show him the way to arrange for his people to worship Him.

Then, he went downstairs and asked to see the manager. In a couple of minutes, a handsome, distinguished looking man came out and introduced himself. He said, "Good morning, I'm David Navarro. How can I help you?"

Monty said, "Hi David, I'm Monty Shepherd."

"Oh yes, you're the one who has reopened the San Sorento Clothing Company. When I found out you were staying with us, I planned to look you up and introduce myself. Thank you very much for staying with us and thank you for bringing your business to San Sorento. Our community needs the jobs. Is there something I can do for you this morning?"

Monty said, "Possibly. David, we have brought almost sixty people over here from Chattanooga to help retrain some of the employees in our new mill, and most of them are accustomed to going to church and worshipping God on Sundays. They are going to be here in San Sorento for nearly six months, and I'm trying to find a place where they can gather and worship, and I was wondering if there would be a possibility that they might use one of your conference rooms once a week for a little over an hour. Of course, I will pay you for it."

"Monty, may I call you Monty?" and Monty said, "of course." "Monty, if your meeting were for anything other than religious meetings, I would let you use our facilities at no charge, but for religious meetings, I have to say I'm sorry, but no. It would just be too risky."

Monty knew why he refused his request, but he asked anyway, "I don't understand. Why would a religious service be too risky?"

"Monty, there is an element here that will not permit anyone to worship anything other than The Church or the First Born of the Lamb of God. You don't have to worship them. You just can't worship anything else as long as you live in what they call their jurisdiction. Even if a person doesn't worship them, they have to pay a tithe to them, and if that person tries to worship something else, the church considers that person a sinner, and he or she is eligible for what they call blood atonement, which could be as serious as death."

"What if we had police protection at our meetings?"

"That might help for that meeting, but it won't help for the next day or two days from then."

"David, what do you think would happen if we held worship services at our own plant?"

"I don't know, Monty. Maybe nothing, but I would be afraid to chance it."

"You know what, David. We have spent a lot of money to get this plant reopened down here, and we can also spend a lot of money taking it away."

"I sure hope you don't do that, Monty."

"Well, I'm telling you, it might just happen."

When he finished talking to David, he went back up to his room and called Bimo.

When Bimo answered, Monty said, "Bimo. Do

you think you can get me an appointment with President Putra?"

"I think I can. When do you want it?"

"As soon as possible. This afternoon, tomorrow or whenever he can see me. It's very urgent that I see him."

"Okay, Monty, I'll call his office right now."

"I'm in my room at the hotel. Call me right back and let me know what he says."

"Okay. Is something wrong, Monty?"

"Yeah, there's plenty wrong. Call the president and call me right back," and he hung up.

Bimo was alarmed by Monty's tone and attitude, and he thought he had better do what he said without questions. He called President Putra's office and set up an appointment with him for Monty.

The caller ID on Monty's phone showed Bimo Flores when it rang, and when Monty picked up, he didn't say "Hello" or any other pleasantries. He answered by asking, "Did you get me an appointment with the president?"

Bimo said, "Yes sir. I made an appointment for you at nine o'clock tomorrow morning. Is that alright?"

Monty didn't answer him. He just said, "Thank you, Bimo," and hung up.

Bimo was going to ask him if he wanted him to go to the president's office with him, but he hung up so fast that he didn't have the chance, and he didn't want to call him back.

Monty spent the rest of the day driving all over the island to see if he could see any buildings that would make a good meeting place. After an exhausting search and not finding anything, he went back to the hotel, changed his clothes and went out to the pool.

Bimo spent the rest of the day worrying because he knew something bad must be wrong or Monty wouldn't be so sharp with his answers when he asked him something. He wondered why he was so anxious to see the president. He thought to himself, *you just don't go to the president with normal problems. They have to be something big.*

The next morning, Monty went downstairs, early, to the dining room at the hotel and had breakfast, then went back to his room and got ready to go see the president of San Sorento. He didn't remember just how long it took to get there when he went with Bimo, so he left at eight thirty, thinking that was more than enough time.

He was right. He pulled into the parking lot, where the president's office was at eight fifty, and by the time he walked into the building and told the receptionist who he was and what he wanted it was nine o'clock. Before he could get to a chair to sit down, President Putra's assistant called his name and said, "The President will see you now."

He thanked her and followed her down the hall to the president's office. When he got to the door, President Putra said, "Good morning, Monty. How are you this fine day?"

"I'm fine, Mr. President. Thank you for asking."

"I know you didn't come up here to pass the time of day. Do you have a problem that I can help you with, Monty?"

"I hope so, Mr. President. Before I tell you what the problem is, let me ask you something. Mr. President, do you believe in God?"

The president was taken aback, and he asked Monty, "Why would you ask me such a question, and to answer you, yes, I believe there is a God."

"I don't mean to offend you, Mr. President, but I didn't ask you if you believed there is a God, I asked you if you believed IN God."

Acting slightly irritated, he asked, "What's the difference? Why are you asking me these questions, Monty? I'm very busy this morning, so please get to your point."

"Sorry, but here's the reason I came here this morning. Mr. President, I have to tell you that I believe in God, and I believe in His Son, Jesus Christ. When I was first approached by Bimo to reopen the San Sorento Clothing Company, I was not interested, but after seeing the plant and its potential, I prayed to God that He would guide me in making my decision, and I prayed that He would help us set things up and help us in every aspect of reopening the closed plant. Everything seemed to fall into place so easily, that I was convinced that it was God's work that allowed it.

"Now, Mr. President, you may or may not know that I have brought almost sixty people over here from our Chattanooga plant to help train the employees of the new Shepherd Apparel/ San Sorento plant. Most of them, and I'm sure, not all of them are also believers in God, and they are used to going to church to worship Him every Sunday. Now, these people are going to be here for around six months, and I want to find a place for them to worship. I haven't seen any churches over here, so I contacted a couple of places to rent a place where we could hold services each week, but in both cases, I was refused because the people over here are so afraid of the Church of the First Born of the Lamb of God. Were you aware of this?"

President Putra answered, "I'm not too familiar with what you're saying, but I have heard of it. Why are you telling me this, Monty?"

"Because, Mr. President, if your people are going to prevent my people from worshipping God, I will close the Shepherd Apparel/ San Sorento plant and take everything back to Chattanooga. I'm sure you have checked out our financial situation, and you know we can easily afford to do that, but I don't want to do it. I just want to be able to find somewhere for my people to be able to worship without fear of being harmed or even killed, but if I can't, two weeks from today, I'll do what I just said I'll do.

Mr. President, I prayed about this yesterday, and I believe He told me to come see you; that you could do something about the situation. Do you think you can?"

"Monty, I'm sure going to try. As soon as you leave, I'll call Chief Guido Vasquez to come to my office, and between the two of us and our entire legislature, we'll try to take care of the situation. Where will you be for the next few days?"

"I'll be here at least until the weekend, but if there are any promising things happening in this regard, I can stay until sometime next week. I don't want this to sound like a threat, but if there are no promising signs by the end of next week, I will take our people home and begin packing up all our materials."

"Monty, I appreciate you coming here this morning. We certainly don't want you to go, and I will assure you that we will do everything in our power to correct this situation. Do I have your phone number?"

"I don't know, sir. Here it is," and he gave him his number and said, "Also, if you can't reach me on my phone, you might try the Holiday Shores Hotel. That's where I'm staying, and Bimo usually knows where I am, so I shouldn't be hard to reach." He got up and shook hands with the president, and as he was leaving, he said, "I surely hope you will be able to do something about this problem. I would really hate to leave," and then he smiled and said, "I'm just beginning to feel at home over here."

He left and returned to his room at the hotel, and about an hour after he got back, his phone rang. The caller ID said, 'San Sorento Govt', and he answered it. When he said hello, the voice on the other end said,

"Monty, this is Arin Putra. How're you doing?"

"I'm fine, Mr. President. How are you?"

"Monty, after you left me earlier, I called Guido Vasquez, the Chief of our legislature, and asked him to come over here. I explained your problem to him, and I emphasized that it was also our problem. Guido was more familiar with it than I was, and he feels that it's time to end the whole thing. He told me that The Church of the First Born of the Lamb of God was actually no longer in existence; that it had ceased to exist in Mexico several years ago, and the people up here that still go along with their teachings are strictly on their own. They have no right to threaten anybody with blood atonement or to collect tithes from them.

"He is calling a special emergency meeting of the Legislature tomorrow morning to try to squelch the movement. We both feel that you have every right to hold worship gatherings, and we will put the full force of the government behind that right, and will severely prosecute anyone that tries to punish anyone else for worshipping their own God.

"After the Legislature meets tomorrow, I'll call you and fill you in on what they did. Monty, I'm very sorry about this and hopefully, the Government of San Sorento will be able to solve your problem."

"Thank you so much, Mr. President. I felt that if anybody could take care of this, it would be you. By the way, if we are successful in getting to hold our services, I would like to invite you to attend some of them. We don't pressure anyone to become a

Christian. We only tell them about what Jesus has done for us and what he can and will do for you, if you will only accept Him to be your Savior. Thank you again, Mr. President. I'll anxiously look forward to your call, tomorrow."

"Goodbye, Monty."

He felt better after talking to President Putra and decided he would go to the Italiano Restaurante for supper. Once, when he went there with Bimo, he had the eggplant parmesan, and it was outstanding, so he thought he would order it again. When he got there, and when they were leading him to his table, he looked up, and lo and behold, Bimo and Sofia were sitting at a table just short of his. He paused to speak to them, and then went on to his table. He kinda thought they might ask him to join them, but they didn't. Bimo looked happy to be on a date, but Sofia looked a little sheepish when she saw him. She might have thought that he wouldn't approve of the two of them together, since they were both his employees. Bimo had asked him about it earlier, but he must not have told Sofia.

They finished before he did, and when they got up to leave, they turned toward him and threw up their hands and left. After they had gone, Monty wondered, *I wonder where dating couples go and what do they do in this little, out of the way place. They can go to a club, but I don't know if either one of them drinks. Oh well, it's none of my business.* It was still early when he finished eating, so he went back to the hotel and sat by the pool until time to go to bed.

Chapter Nine

Monty was kind of nervous when he got up the next morning. He knew the Legislature was going to be in a called emergency meeting around ten o'clock, and he knew he didn't have any control over what was going to happen. He just hoped and prayed that President Puta did a good enough job on the Chief of the Legislature to do a good job on the legislators.

He showered and got dressed and went downstairs for breakfast. When he finished, he didn't want to just sit in the room waiting for President Putra's call, so he got into the Suburban and drove down to the plant. When he walked in, it looked as if everybody was busy with their individual jobs, and he noticed that some of the Chattanooga trainers were actually running sewing machines, while others were standing next to the operators, showing them how to do something. He walked back to the inspection department, and everybody was busy as were the packers. Several large nylon hampers were full of garments that had been packed and were waiting to be put in their boxes. Beyond that were the people who put the individual boxes in the shipping boxes to fill the orders. From there, the garments were put in large shipping containers and put on pallets to await shipping.

He went from there back into the plant and over to

the cutting department, where Bill had added two additional cutters and three cloth spreaders. He was planning to add two more cutters and possibly three more spreaders because it takes a lot of manpower to hand-spread and cut three thousand dozen garments every day. With the addition of the next two cutters and three spreaders, the cutting department should be fully staffed with five cutters and eight spreaders.

Monty stood and watched for several minutes, and in a little bit, Bill Glasser finished cutting the order he was working on, and he waved and spoke to Monty. Monty went over to him, and they talked for a couple of minutes. While he was talking to Bill, his phone rang. The caller ID said San Sorento Govt. Monty excused himself and answered, "This is Monty. Good morning."

The voice on the other end said, "Mr. Shepherd, please hold for President Putra."

Monty said, "Thank you."

In about two seconds, the president got on the phone. "Good morning, Monty. This is Arin Putra."

He looked over at Bill and smiled and said, "Good morning, Mr. President. How are you?"

"I'm fine, Monty. I wanted to call you and tell you that the Legislature met this morning and overwhelmingly ruled that there will be no more threats or persecution of any religious groups seeking to worship, and we are going to notify every citizen of this ruling. Two days from now, we should have enough flyers printed to notify every household in

San Sorento. We are going to enlist as many as it takes to hand deliver the flyers, so everyone will know about it by the weekend. Do you plan to hold services this Sunday?"

"Mr. President, we'd sure like to, but we still don't have a place to hold it. Maybe, with your new ruling, we can find someone relaxed enough to let us hold them at their place. I'm going out this afternoon and search for a location. Mr. President, would the government happen to own any place that's vacant where we could hold services until we can find a place?"

"I don't know, at this point, Monty, but I'll check with the head of our land and grounds department. What kind of building do you need?"

"It doesn't have to be very big. If my people are the only ones attending, then a building with three or four thousand square feet will do, but if we should be lucky enough to get some San Sorentoans to attend, I'd say we will probably need about five thousand feet, and of course, we will need benches or chairs for that many. That's one reason I asked the Dunes and the Holiday Shores Hotel because their conference rooms would be equipped with seating. In years past, Mr. President, did San Sorento not ever have a church of any kind? I would be very surprised if there weren't some Catholic Churches somewhere."

"Monty, I'll have to check on that. Give me a couple of days to get things started and maybe we can find what you need."

"Thank you, Mr. President."

He hung up and told Bill, "Bill, I'm having a heck of a time finding a place for our group to have church services."

"Really? I thought that would be a snap."

"No, it's not. Everybody down here is scared to death to have any kind of religious meeting in public. They think that if they do, then they might get burned out or maybe even killed."

"You don't mean it. Who would've thought?"

"I'll tell you about it when we have some time. I've been so upset about it, I went to the president of San Sorento. That was who I was talking to just a few minutes ago. I told him that if we couldn't worship down here, that we would pack everything up, close the plant and go back to Chattanooga, and we weren't going to wait. When he saw I meant it, he called the head of the Legislature, and they called a special emergency meeting of the Legislature this morning to try and resolve things with their people. He tried to assure me on the phone that everything is going to be alright, so we'll see. He said the government is having flyers printed, and in a couple of days, they will be hand delivered to every citizen of San Sorento."

"Monty, were you serious about closing the plant and going back to Chattanooga?"

"I was as serious as a heart attack. We'll stay one more week, and if things aren't resolved by then, then that's it."

"Wow. Monty, I knew you packed a lot of power, but I didn't realize that you packed enough to stare down an entire country." He said, "Remind me to keep you on my side."

Monty smiled and said, "I guess I'll leave now. Bill, how about not saying anything about what we just talked about. I would like to give President Putra time to work things out if he can, and if he can, and we get to freely worship, then we can tell the story. Also, Bill, I know I asked you to lead the services, and you said you would, but I didn't know I was going to have this kind of trouble. If we're able to get things worked out, would you mind if I led the first service?"

"No, Boss. I would very much appreciate it if you would."

"Okay. I'll see you. Remember, mums the word."

As he was walking up through the sewing room, on his way out of the plant, he ran into Sofia. They both smiled, and Monty said, "Hi Sofia. Did you have a good time last night?"

"Yes sir."

"Are you going to see Bimo again?"

"Tonight."

Monty said, "Wow," and kept walking. He went back to the hotel and after he ate lunch, he changed clothes and went down to the pool and sat in one of their comfortable chaise lounges. After a while, in between naps, he called Joan. When she answered, he said, "Hey Sugar. What are you doing?"

"I'm just sitting here, wishing you were here. When are you coming home?"

"That's why I called. I have run into a situation down here that was completely unexpected, and I may have to be here for at least another week after this week. We're having two planes a week coming down here and I was wondering if you might want to hitch a ride on one of them and come down here. I sure would like to see you."

"What kind of situation?"

"I don't want to get into the whole thing over the phone, but it has to do with finding a place for our people to worship on Sundays. We're facing opposition, and I'm trying to get it worked out. I've been able to get President Putra involved, and it looks as though we may be able to get things worked out, but it's going to take several more days, and I'd sure like to see you."

"How do I go about catching one of the planes?"

"You don't have to do a thing. Call Jimmy, and he'll take care of everything."

"When do you want me to come?"

"Yesterday."

"Seriously, when do you want me to come?"

"Just as quick as you feel like you can. I have forgotten the exact plane schedule, but I think it will be here either Saturday or Sunday. Check with Jimmy. He'll know. You don't have to rush, but I sure wish you would. Think about it and call Jimmy, and then let me know."

"What are you doing right now?"

"I'm working really hard. I talked to the President earlier and had to come back to the hotel and take a nap. I just woke up to call you, and I have to hurry and hang up so I can take another nap before supper."

"It sounds like you're working really hard. Okay, I'll come this weekend if I can catch the plane."

"Good girl. Be sure to bring your suit. The weather is great."

After he talked to Joan, his mood was much brighter, and he had an idea. He thought he would go downstairs and tell David Navarro about his talk with the president and the president's call to him, telling him about the Legislature's emergency meeting, and what they decided. He hoped that would change his mind about not allowing a religious service to be held at the hotel.

He changed from his bathing suit back into his street clothes and caught the elevator down to the lobby. When he got to the desk, he asked to see Mr. Navarro, and the clerk said he was gone for the day. That disappointed him, and he went back up to his room. Then, he decided he would call Bimo. When Bimo saw the caller ID, he answered, "Hi Monty."

"Hi Bimo, I want to ask you something. You were born here in San Sorento, weren't you?"

"Yes sir. I was."

"Well, do you remember ever seeing a church, probably a Catholic Church, when you were a little boy?"

"Off hand, I don't remember seeing one, but let me think back and try to jog my memory. Can I call you back?"

"Yeah. Call me if you remember anything."

He didn't call back that day, so Monty figured he didn't remember anything. He probably had his mind on his upcoming date that night with Sofia Perez.

Bimo had asked Monty about his seeing Sofia, and Monty told him that there was no company policy against fraternalization that he knew of, so he took that as an okay. Still, he and Sofia didn't want to flaunt their relationship, so she would walk out front of the Dunes and down the street a little when it was time for him to pick her up. They didn't try to hide their relationship; they just didn't want to advertise it.

That evening, Bimo picked her up at that spot and at his suggestion, they went to the Pargo Rojo, a chicken and seafood restaurant with a nice atmosphere. On their first date, the night before, most of what they talked about was work and how things were going at the plant, but that evening, he wanted to know more about her personal life, so he asked questions after they ordered their food. He said, "Honey, why don't you tell me something about yourself?

She asked, "What do you want to know?"

He said, "You know, we talk a lot alike. Where are you from?"

"I'm from Chattanooga, Tennessee."

"No, I mean originally."

"I was born in La Gloria, Nueva Leon, Mexico, and when I was a young girl, we moved to Laredo, Texas."

"Were your parents legal or illegal?"

"They were legal. Daddy worked for a large manufacturing plant in Mexico, and his company transferred him to Laredo. After about a year and a half or two years, he got his Green Card and later, he and my mother got their United States citizenship. The company he worked for made huge excavators and machines like that, and they had another company in Chattanooga that was even larger than the one in Laredo. Daddy had done good work for them and after we had been in Laredo three or four years, they transferred him to Chattanooga, and that's where I live now."

"Do your parents still live there?"

"Mama does, but Daddy died three years ago."

"I'm sorry to hear that. Do you have any brothers or sisters?"

"I have one younger sister."

"Have you ever been married?"

"No, but I almost got married one time."

"What happened?"

"He got cold feet and canceled the wedding."

"Do you still see him?"

"Bimo, if you don't mind, I don't want to talk about it."

"Okay. Sorry."

Sofia said, "Now that you know everything about me, tell me about you. Are you from here?"

"There's not much to tell. Yes, I was born here. I went to school here, and after I got out of school, I went to work for the San Sorento Clothing Company, and I've been here ever since. My parents are both gone, and I have one sister. That's my story in a nutshell."

They finished their dinner and Bimo wanted to show her some of the sights of San Sorento, so they went south of the main population to an area that was almost a wilderness and took a walk on the beach. The moon wasn't full, but it almost was, and every star in the sky seemed to be overlooking the San Sorento beach. It all made for a very romantic mood, and Bimo, especially, intended to take full advantage of it. At one point, they stopped and took off their shoes and then walked in the edge of the warm water. They walked without talking for a good while, and then Bimo stopped, turned toward Sofia and turned her toward him and kissed her. He was happy when she didn't turn away, but returned the kiss.

Neither said a word, but continued walking. They walked for maybe a half a mile, stopping every few minutes to kiss. After the fourth or fifth kiss, Bimo said, "This is amazing, but I think we need to head back. Maybe we can come back another night and bring a picnic and a blanket."

Sofia said, "That sounds wonderful," and gave him a special kiss.

Not much was said on the way back, and both of them were in a state of euphoria. When they got to the car, they had to put their shoes on, but they had to get the sand off their feet first, and they both mumbled while they were doing it. Finally, they were ready, and they got in the car and headed back to town. On the way, Bimo asked, "Are you up to going out with me again?"

"I certainly am. When?"

"I'm free tomorrow night. How about you?"

"Yep. I'm free, too."

"You want to do the picnic that I mentioned?"

"If you want to. It would sure be different from what I'm used to. I think it would be fun."

Soon they reached the Dunes, and Sofia got out down the street at the same place where Bimo picked her up. They kissed goodnight and said they would see each other the next morning. There were still some people at the pool, including Champak, and Sofia went over and joined her until almost everybody got up and went in. Before they went in, however, Champak asked, "Did you go out with Bimo tonight?"

"Yes, and it was wonderful."

"What did you all do?"

"Well, first we went to eat at the Pargo Rojo, and the food was delicious. We talked a lot of personal talk, and then we went for a ride and went way down south where there were no people and walked on the beach. It was ultra romantic, and we had a great time."

"Did anything happen?"

"What do you mean?"

"Well, you said it was ultra romantic, so did anything happen?"

"Not what you think, but he kissed me."

"Did you kiss him back?"

"What do you think? All right, let's go up to our apartment."

"You did, didn't you?"

"Yes, now hush up about it."

The next day was a normal day. After everyone showed up, Sofia spent the morning teaching two women how to hem the bottoms of shirts, and Bimo was busy trying to show Luiz Garza different things about being a plant manager. Every now and then, Sofia and Bimo's eyes would meet when he would come by where she was, but nothing was said. It was strictly a work environment. At lunch, he looked her up, and when he found her, he said, "I hate to have to tell you this, but I'm going to have to cancel tonight. My sister called, and she has a problem, and I'm going to have to go over there when I get off this afternoon. I doubt if I'll be through in time for us to do anything tonight. I am so sorry."

"Sofia said, "No problem. We'll do something another time. Don't worry about it."

Bimo was still helping shuttle the Chattanooga women to work and back, and that afternoon, Sofia rode in his van. When they got to the Dunes, as she was getting out, he said, "Tomorrow's Saturday.

Want to have that picnic tomorrow? It should be a good day for it."

"Yeah. Call me," she said.

After Monty ate supper, he walked up to the Dunes to see if he could see any of his people outside, and there weren't many, but he picked out a couple or three and sat down with them, just to be sociable. He had hoped to see Bill Glasser and talk about the Sunday devotions, but Bill wasn't outside when he got there. He was almost ready to get up and start back to his hotel when Bill came out with Patrick Haynes.

They didn't see him at first, then when he got up, they did, and they pointed to some vacant chairs and motioned for him. He went over and the three of them sat down, and talked generally about how things were going at the plant and how they were liking San Sorento.

Bill said, "Monty, you said you were going to tell me about that call you got from the president."

"I did, didn't I. Well, I won't tell all of it because we'd be here 'til midnight if I try, but I can give you the basics, and I'd like for you to keep it under your hat right now, okay?"

Bill said, "Okay."

"Patrick?"

"Yes sir. I won't say a word."

"Bill, remember when I asked you if you would lead the devotions for our folks on Sunday mornings, after I found a place to have them?"

"Yes sir. I remember."

"Well, I think I started looking for a place either that day or the day after, and right here at the Dunes was my first stop. When I asked Pablo about it, he said he was sorry, but no. It was too dangerous. I questioned him about that, and he told me that there is an element here that won't permit any kind of religious services to be held. He said if he let us meet here, that the Dunes would possibly be burned out or maybe some people even killed. I left Pablo and went to the Holiday Shores, where I'm staying, and asked David Navarro, the manager, the same thing, and I got the same answer. There is a group here known as The Church of the First Born of the Lamb of God, and they are vicious. I decided to do something about it if I could, so I got an appointment with President Putra, and I told him that if we could not worship God here, then I would close the plant and move all our people back to Chattanooga, and all his people would be out of jobs again. I gave him two weeks to take care of it or we're gone.

"He saw that I was serious, so he called Guido Vasquez, the Chief of the San Sorento Legislature and told him what I was going to do, and Guido called a special emergency meeting of the Legislature, and hopefully, they're going to do something about it. That call I got from the president when I was with you was him telling me what the government of San Sorento was going to do."

"What's he going to do, Monty?"

"First of all, the Legislature ruled that there can be no suppression or persecution of any religion in San Sorento. They are having enough flyers printed right now to reach every citizen in the country, and they are going to have as many people as it takes to hand deliver the flyers, so no one can say they didn't get one. Once, the people get the flyers and know what the government has said, if anyone or any group makes it hard on any religious meeting, they will have to answer to the government. I will probably be talking to President Putra tomorrow or Monday, and we'll just have to see what happens."

"Are you going to continue to try and find a place for us to meet?"

"Absolutely. I told the president that I felt pretty sure that there are several obsolete church buildings in San Sorento, and I wish he would locate one for us. He said he would try. I think I scared him when I told him what we were going to do, so I feel good that he will come up with something. He knows they only have next week to solve our problem, so I believe he'll do something. Bill, Patrick, if you will, please pray about this. I have spent a ton of money trying to get this thing off the ground, and I sure hate to lose it, but if it separates us from God, I'm going to do it in a heartbeat. Guys, this has been nice, but I guess I'll head back to my hotel now. As I said earlier, please keep this under your hat for now. I don't want everybody knowing about this until the government gets everything taken care of. I'll see you in the morning. Good night."

After he left, Bill asked Patrick, "How many other CEOs do you know that would do something like that? Not only is he a CEO, but he's one of the most powerful CEOs in the country. There aren't too many that would call the president and threaten him if he didn't do what he wanted. Patrick, I think we're pretty lucky to work for such a guy."

"You've got that right," Patrick said.

The next morning, Saturday, Monty's phone rang, and it was President Putra. "Good morning, Mr. President," Monty said.

"Good morning, Monty. How are you this morning?"

"I'm fine, sir. How are you?"

"I'm good. I just wanted to tell you where we are right now. First, we are not quite through printing all the flyers yet, but we finished a lot yesterday and began delivering them last night. We should be through printing later today, and by Monday, they should all be delivered. Second, I think I might have found you a building that you can use for your services."

"Really? Tell me about it.

The president gave him the address and then said, "That is a store building that is no longer in business, and the electricity and air conditioning is still connected. There are plenty of chairs at our convention center that you can use, and we'll bring them to you. I think tomorrow will probably be too soon to use the building because everybody won't have the flyers yet, and it might still be too dangerous to try and have your meeting there, but I have come up with an alternative for tomorrow."

"What is that, Mr. President?"

"I talked to Guido about this, and we think we would like to offer you the chance to use the conference room in the Capitol, tomorrow. There is plenty of seating, and it's very comfortable. Does that sound like something you would be interested in?"

"Wow, Mr. President. You just can't know how much I appreciate this."

"Will your people be able to get to the Capitol?"

"I think so. We have two vans plus two other vehicles. I don't know how many will come on this short notice, but we'll make it happen. We won't meet until around ten o'clock, and that will give us time to make three or four trips if we need to."

"Maybe I can help you with that. The San Sorento Public Works Department has a tour bus that it uses in high season and is not being used right now. We can loan that to you, if you would like. I think it will carry about forty people."

"It just keeps getting better, Mr. President. Thank you. We would love to use the tour bus.

"Great. I'll have my Assistant set it all up for you, and she will give you a call later this afternoon to confirm everything."

"Thank you so much, Mr. President."

"You're welcome, and before we hang up, when we're in private, I'd like for you to call me Arin. In public, you can still call me Mr. President, but I feel as if we've become friends, and I'd like for you call me Arin. Okay?"

"Okay, Arin. I like that. Thank you."

As soon as he hung up from the president, he made a beeline up to the Dunes to see as many of his people as he could find. Fortunately, it was a beautiful day, and most of them were already outside; either by the pool or at the beach. He wanted Bill to sort of take charge, but he wasn't outside yet, so Monty went to his door and knocked. When he came to the door, Monty said, "Bill, I just finished talking to the president, and he arranged for us to have a church service tomorrow in a safe place, and I'd like to tell our people about it. Would you mind helping me get everybody together so I can talk to them for about five minutes? We'll just gather by the pool, and I promise it won't take but a few short minutes."

It took about ten minutes for everybody to get together because a lot of them were still indoors when Monty wanted to talk to them and going door to door took time. When they were all gathered and giving their attention to Monty, he said, "Good morning. I hope you've all had a good week. The reason I wanted to talk to you this morning is to tell you something that you've probably been wondering about. I know that most of you are used to going to church every Sunday, and there are no churches in San Sorento for you to go to. I talked to Bill Glasser about it and he graciously accepted my invitation to lead you in worship every Sunday while we're here. The only problem was we didn't have any idea where we could meet. After looking on my own and not being successful finding a place, I resorted to an extreme. I went straight to the president of San Sorento. He understood our problem and said he would help us find a place. He called me a few minutes ago and offered to let us worship in the conference room at the Capitol, tomorrow only, and he even offered to furnish a tour bus owned by the government. After tomorrow, he said there is an empty store building we can use as long as we're here. I just wanted to tell you this, so if you want to go worship God as a group, there is a way. I thought that ten o'clock, tomorrow morning would be a good time, so that's what I told President Putra. I hope you will all take advantage of this because you can't imagine what I had to go through to get this far. Bill has said that I can deliver the first message, and after that, he will lead you, so please pray about it and please support your fellow workers by worshipping with them. Thank you all for listening. Have a great day in the sun, today."

Chapter Ten

Just as soon as Monty finished talking to his people, Sofia's phone rang. It was Bimo. She said, "Good morning."

"Good morning. It looks like a good day for a picnic. What do you think?"

"It looks that way from here."

"Would you rather have a lunch picnic or a dinner picnic?"

"I don't care. Which would you rather have?"

"I would prefer a dinner picnic, but in this case, I think I would rather have a lunch picnic because that way, I can be with you longer."

He picked her up around eleven o'clock, and they drove to the area where they went a couple of nights ago. Sofia wore her suit with a cute coverup and flipflops. She had on sunglasses and carried a bag with sunscreen and other things in it. With that outfit and her cute figure, she looked like a million dollars, or in this case, seventeen million, sixty-four hundred thousand, and five hundred pesos. Bimo wore his trunks and had on a printed t-shirt. He also wore flipflops. They found a place to spread their blanket close to where they were the other night, but this time, there were other people around them.

Bimo asked, "What have you been doing this morning?"

"Not much. This is laundry day, so I had to strip the bed and take the sheets and towels and things to the area where they do the washing and drying. About nine or nine thirty Monty Shepherd came up to the Dunes and talked to all of us about going to church tomorrow. It seems that he was able to somehow get the conference room at the Capitol to hold the meeting, and President Putra is sending a tour bus to pick up whoever wants to go."

"Are you going?"

"I think I will. Why don't you go with me?"

"You don't want me to go, besides, I'm not one of you from Chattanooga."

"You don't have to be. The meeting is open to everybody. It's a church meeting where you learn about God and Jesus. I've heard that Bill Glasser is going to be the regular leader, but tomorrow, Monty Shepherd is going to lead. Monty's a good speaker It should be good. Come go with me."

"Speaking of church meetings, as I was leaving home somebody handed me a flyer. The guy said he and a bunch of other people have to give one to every citizen of San Sorento by this weekend. It has to do with church meetings, and after what you said Monty told you, this has Monty Shepherd written all over it."

"What did it say?"

"It said something to the effect that 'effective immediately, any suppression or persecution of any religious person or group is absolutely forbidden. If anyone or any group is caught suppressing or persecuting any religion, they will be prosecuted to the full extent of the law. Violation of this ordinance will carry a fine for the first offense of eighty thousand Pesos or three years in prison or both. A second offense will carry a fine of one hundred seventy-three thousand Pesos or five years in prison or both. Suppression or persecution of any religion in San Sorento will not be tolerated. Any violation cannot be appealed.' It was signed Arin Putra, President of the Commonwealth of San Sorento and Guido Vasquez, Chief of Legislature, Commonwealth of San Sorento."

Sofia said, "It sounds like they mean business."

"It does, doesn't it?"

Bimo had spent a long time cooking the night before their picnic, and since it was so close to lunchtime when they got to the beach, they ate soon after they spread their blanket and got things sort of organized. He had made a wonderful guacamole and he had also made some delicious Tacos de Carnitas with a Salsa Verde. To top it all off, he made a large pitcher of Margaritas, which they sipped on most of the afternoon.

He had made so much food, they ate their fill at lunch and still had a lot left over for supper, so they didn't have to go to a restaurant,

The day was perfect. Not only did they get to spend most of it together, they were able to talk enough to really get inside the other's being as well as sneaking a kiss from time to time. Sofia was exhausted by the time they ate their supper, and she asked Bimo to take her home around eight o'clock. Before she left him, she made him promise that he would go to church with her the next day.

Monty walked up to the Dunes the next morning to catch a ride on the tour bus for the trip to the Capitol for their church meeting. He had worked quite a bit on his talk the night before, and he just hoped he would be able to say some things that might make a difference in their lives.

He was hoping that all fifty seven would go that morning, and he knew, deep down, that that would not happen, but counting him, there were forty seven on the bus, and Bimo and Sofia made forty nine total.

As he got off the bus, he invited the driver, who could not speak English, so he saw Champak Sandoval getting off the bus, and he asked her if she would be a translator, if he could get the bus driver to attend. She agreed, and she asked the driver if he would come in, and he did. Champak stood up front and translated as Monty talked.

Everyone sat and talked when they first got inside, and in just a few minutes, he tapped on the podium to get their attention, and the first thing he did was lead them in prayer and after the prayer, he read from the book of John. The scripture he read was John three, verses one through sixteen.

He began his message by saying, "I'm sure glad to see all of you this morning. I'm sure you have no idea what we had to go through in order to get here. When I talked to you about coming to San Sorento, before we left Chattanooga, I told you that I asked God to help us if He wanted us to come. After a lot of prayer, things began to fall into place, and I was sure it was God telling me to go ahead and get ready, which we did. After we got ready to open the plant, and after you all got over here, it dawned on me that I had not made any preparations for us to worship, and those of you who are used to going to church every Sunday should not be kept from worshipping for six months. I was scheduled to go back to Chattanooga last week, but when I realized that I had not prepared a place for you to worship, I sent Jimmy on home, and I told him I was going to stay until I found a place. I went to two large tourist venues and asked if we could rent a conference room or somewhere in their place to hold religious meetings, and they both turned us down. It seems that there has been a violent cult in San Sorento that has put fear into everybody that attempts to worship anything but The Church of the First Born of the Lamb of God. The managers of both places I went refused to let us meet at their place for the same reason. They said they were afraid that they might be burned out or even killed. I didn't know who those people were, so I asked my friend Bimo if he knew them, and he did.

"What he told me was bone chilling. Those people thought nothing of killing, even their own children. They were mixed up in crime, and if you crossed them, you were guilty of sinning against them, and you were subject to what they called 'blood atonement', which is another term for murder.

"After hearing these things, the only thing I could think of was to go to the top, so I asked Bimo to get me an appointment with the president of San Sorento, which he did. The other day, I met with President Putra and told him that if we couldn't worship God over here, that we would close the plant, lay everybody off, and go back to Chattanooga. I gave him two weeks to solve the problem.

After my visit with him, he called in Guido Vasquez, the Chief of the Legislature, and they agreed to crack down on these people. They have printed out flyers and are or have already hand delivered them to every citizen of San Sorento, outlining the fact that no one or no group is allowed to suppress or persecute any other religious group. If anyone is caught doing it, they will be fined, in American terms, five thousand dollars or three years in prison, or both, for the first offense, and ten thousand dollars or five years in prison, or both, for a second offense.

"President Putra called me Friday and told me what they were going to do, and he's the one who allowed us to meet in here this morning, and he is the one who arranged for the bus we used. One more thing he did. When he called me, he said he had found a vacant building for us to use. I haven't seen it yet, but if the president says it's a good building for us to use, then I feel confident that it will be a good building.

"Now, I've taken a lot of time this morning, talking about things that are not Biblical, but in a sense, they are. You have been put in an ideal situation where you can become missionaries without even trying. There is possibly not one Christian in this country, and each one of you is working next to around four hundred and fifty unsaved people eight hours every day. You don't have to preach to them. You might simply tell somebody that you went to church this morning, and if they ask you what you did, you can say, 'we learned about Jesus,' or you can ask them, 'do you know who Jesus is?' You don't have to have a prepared talk in order to witness to them.

"In the book of Mark, Mark 16, Jesus says, 'Go into all the world and preach the gospel.' This is something each of you can do without even trying. Just carry on a conversation with someone you're working with and steer the conversation to your going to church. I have one more thing, and then I'll be through. If you're able to lead any of these people to Jesus, let Bill Glasser know, and he will let me know, and for anyone who wants to accept Jesus or even learn about Him, I will send them a Bible. It doesn't matter how many. Folks, this could be something greater than you ever thought of.

"Before we close, are there any comments?"

"Bimo stood up and said, "I have something. As I was leaving home, yesterday morning, somebody gave me one of the flyers you talked about. Also, I want to learn more about Jesus. Will you tell me about him?"

Monty said, "I absolutely will. Why don't you come to my hotel this afternoon, and we'll talk. Anybody else have anything? If not, bow your heads and let's thank God."

When he finished praying, he thanked everybody for being there and told them Bill would be leading them next week. He said, "Why don't each one of you try to bring at least one more person with you? Can you imagine how pleased God would be about that?"

On the way back to the Dunes, the bus turned at a place that was not familiar ro Monty, but he didn't say anything. In a few minutes Alvaro pulled over and stopped. He turned around and said, "The president wanted me to show you this building. This is where he said you can meet after today."

After church, Sofia and Bimo stopped by the Pueblo Grill and got a cheeseburger. While they were in the restaurant, Sofia asked Bimo, "Bimo, what did you think about our meeting?"

"I liked what Monty said. I'm going to go to his hotel and talk to him this afternoon. Are you one of those, what he called, Christians?"

"Yeah, I am."

"Well, after I talk to Monty this afternoon, maybe I'll be one. He said something that bothered me, though."

"What did he say?"

"He said that if he couldn't find a place to worship

over here, that he would shut everything down and go back to Chattanooga. If this other building doesn't work out and he shuts everything down, will you go back to Chattanooga?"

"I'd have to. Chattanooga is where I live."

"Why couldn't you stay here with me?"

"If I stayed here, what would I do? I wouldn't have a job, and I have to work."

Bimo said, "We'd find you a job."

"Doing what?"

"I don't know, but we'd find something for you."

"If Monty closed the plant, what would you do?"

"I don't know. All I've ever done is work in the clothing plant. I have gotten to know President Putra fairly good, and maybe if I call him, he will give me a job or help me find something. I don't want to think about the plant closing. I feel sure the radicals or former radicals will calm down, now that the government is threatening to put them in prison."

"I hope so, but let's say the plant stays open. Will you miss me when I go home?"

"You can't imagine how much I'll miss you. That's why I want you to stay so much."

"Well, let's think positive and think the plant will stay open, and you'll be tired of me after six months, anyway. Take me to the Dunes now, okay? I don't want you to be late seeing Monty."

After he dropped Sofia off at the Dunes, he went straight to Monty's at the hotel. He knocked on the door, and when Monty opened it, Bimo said, "Hi

Monty. Am I too early?"

"No. Come on in."

When he got inside and sat down, Monty said, "I'm glad you came by, Bimo. You said you had some questions about our worshipping God and Jesus. Is there anything specific that you want to find out about?"

He told Monty that he didn't understand certain things, and Monty tried to explain the answers to him as best he could, and when Bimo seemed to understand them, and said he thought he would like to accept Jesus, Monty prayed with him.

Just as they were finishing talking and praying, Bimo's phone rang. It was Kevin Hart, saying they would be landing in one hour, and would he pick them up at the airport?"

Before Bimo had quite finished talking to Kevin, Monty's phone rang, and it was Joan. She said the same thing Kevin did and asked Monty to pick them up. They both smiled and decided that Monty would be the one to go to the airport.

The big plane landed exactly when Kevin said it would, and Monty was really glad to see Joan. He had had a pretty rough week with the problems having to do with a meeting place, and Joan was always his 'go to' when things were not going smoothly for him.

He took Kevin and Jim Goff, and on this trip, Ed Harris to the Dunes. Ed had come along on this trip because they were ready to load some containers to ship to Jose and Bruno, and Ed could show the new men how to load them. When he dropped them off, he and Joan went to the hotel, where Joan said she was tired and wanted to relax. After she had rested for just a few minutes, Monty said, "Sugar, why don't you get your suit on, and you can rest outside by the pool or we can go down to the beach?"

She thought that sounded good, and she got up and changed into her swimsuit. At the same time, Bimo had gone home and changed into his swimsuit and went to the Dunes and spent time with Sofia.

Chapter Eleven

When Monty and Joan had found chairs at the beach and sat down, Joan said, "Honey, you sounded stressed when you called me to come out here. Is everything alright?"

"I hope so, but a week ago, I was ready to shut our plant down and go home."

"Why, what happened?"

"Well, I didn't want to worry you, so I didn't say anything to you, but when I tried to find a place to use for our temporary church, I was met with warnings of being burned out, all the way to being murdered. I prayed hard about it, and I decided I couldn't lose anything, so I got an appointment with President Putra, and at our meeting, I told him in no uncertain terms, that if I couldn't find a place in San Sorento for my people to worship, I would close the plant and lay everybody off. I gave him two weeks to come up with a solution, and hopefully, he has come up with something. He has found us a building, and it looks pretty good, but I've got to figure out how to get chairs in it. I'm going to call the president tomorrow and see if he has any ideas. I hope he'll say we can borrow some from the government, and while I have him on the phone, I'm going to ask about getting the tour bus, that we used this morning, to take the people to church every Sunday."

"It sounds as if he's trying to help you from what you say."

"I think he is, but it's too early to tell. This morning was our first meeting, and it was held at the Capitol, which was pretty safe, and next week, the meeting will be held at the building I was telling you about. We'll see what happens after that."

Unbeknownst to Monty, several of the folks who were staying at the Dunes grabbed a quick bite and went to the pool, where they talked about the meeting and what Monty had challenged them to do in regard to talking to some of their co-workers about Jesus and asking them to come to church with them. Nearly all of them who were out there said they were going to do that, and instead of forty next week, maybe there would be as many as sixty attending the service.

Monty and Joan soon ran out of anything else to talk about, and they just laid there, looking and listening to the waves. Soon, they were both asleep. Joan went to sleep because she was tired after her trip and Monty went to sleep because, for the first time in several days, he was relaxed, having Joan with him.

The next morning, both of them slept until about seven o'clock, which was late for Monty, and after a leisurely breakfast, they went back up to their room, and Monty got on the phone. He called Bimo first to see if everything got started alright that morning, and he was assured that it did.

He told him, "Bimo, I need to call President Putra, and I don't have his number. How about giving it to me, and you won't have to lead interference for me the way you've had to do before."

"Okay. Hold on a minute while I find it." He was worried that there might still be something upsetting Monty, so he asked, "Is everything alright, Monty?"

"Yeah, I just need to ask him a couple of things."

Bimo gave him the number, and he immediately dialed President Putra. He didn't know it beforehand, but the number Bimo gave him was the president's personal number. After a couple of rings, the president answered, "President Putra."

"Good morning, Arin. Monty Shepherd here."

"Good morning, Monty. How was your meeting, yesterday?"

"Really good. We had a few more than forty people in attendance, and hopefully, there will be more next Sunday. Thank you so much for your help."

"Glad to be of some help."

"Arin, the bus took us by the building on Copa Street yesterday, and it looks very nice, however, there are no chairs or anything for the people to sit on. Would you have any idea where we could get some?"

"I forgot to tell you, Monty. I'm going to have some chairs delivered down there. How many do you think you will need?"

"I hope there will be around sixty there. Would it be asking too much to ask for seventy-five, just in case there are more?"

"Seventy-five it is. Is there anything else I might help you with?"

"Arin, I hate to ask, but none of my people have cars over here. Would it be possible for the tour bus to run again?"

"Absolutely. When I first told you about the bus, I meant for you to use it every time you have your meeting. You must have misunderstood me."

"I must have. Thank you so much. Arin, I need to get back to Chattanooga as soon as I can, and I may leave one day later this week. I doubt I'll be here for next Sunday's meeting, and if you need anything from us, just call Bimo, and he'll take care of whatever you need. Oh, I almost forgot. Arin, we need some keys to the building. When the people deliver the chairs, could they bring us some keys?"

"I'll take care of it. How many will you need?"

"I think three will be plenty. Thanks again, Arin, and if I don't see or talk to you before I leave, we have each other's numbers, so let's be sure to stay in touch."

"Okay, Monty. Good luck."

When he hung up from President Putra, he felt like he needed to go to the plant to see Bimo. He asked Joan to go, and she gladly said she would like to. She didn't know any of the people, even the ones from Chattanooga, so she just tagged along behind Monty and met the ones he introduced her to."

He told Bimo, "I'm going to try to go home later this week, so if there's anything you need for me to do before I go, try to think of it. I talked to President Putra, and he is going to have seventy-five chairs delivered and set up at that building on Copa street, and he's also having three keys sent with the chairs. If I'm not here, you take one, give one to Bill Glasser and hold one for me."

"What day are you leaving?"

"I hope to leave on the next plane, but that's not definite. I don't want to leave until I'm sure everything for our church meetings is taken care of."

"Why don't you stay until next week? You should be at the first church meeting in the new location just to be sure everything is the way you want it."

"You might have something there. Joan might want to stay, so we'll just have us a short vacation."

He and Joan made the best of the few days they had left by relaxing on the beach, sightseeing and other things that tourists do. Now that he had a vehicle to drive, they could go and do whatever they wanted to. They had already seen and done some of the things when they were there before with Jerry and Tracy Martin, but this time was special. They were by themselves and didn't have to worry about anybody but themselves, and that was kinda nice.

Time flew by, and before they knew it, the week was almost gone. On Thursday, Monty thought he would go to the building they were to use for their services to make sure the chairs had been delivered and to pick up his key. He parked out front on the street and when he walked up the short walk to the door, he was horrified by what he saw, and he immediately called President Putra.

The president must have been busy because the phone rang a long time before he answered. Finally, he answered. "President Putra."

"Hi Arin. Monty Shepherd. How are you?"

"Fine, Monty. I thought you had gone back to Tennessee."

"Well, I was going to leave, but I decided to stay over until next week, so I could go to our church service in the new location. I'm here now, and when I got here a few minutes ago, I was shocked to see that someone had built a fire on the sidewalk leading up to the front door. What do you suggest, Arin?"

"Are you there now?"

"Yes sir."

"Well, hang tight. I'm going to come over there. Please wait for me."

"Okay. I'll wait."

In about fifteen minutes the president drove up with his aide, and they got out. About two minutes later, a police car drove up with none other than the Chief of Police and a Captain of the police. They got out and walked over to where Monty, Joan, and the president and his aide were standing. They all spoke, and the president introduced the policemen to Monty and Joan. The Chief's name was Tomas Marin.

They all looked at the ashes and the unburnt wood, and President Putra asked, "What do you make of this, Tomas?"

"Well, Mr. President, since these ashes are the only thing we have to go by, I'd have to say that this is a warning from the First Born of the Lamb group."

"I agree. My question is, what are we going to do about it?" He put his hand on Monty's shoulder and said, "This man has spent a lot of money trying to establish a manufacturing plant, giving a lot of people otherwise unemployed, work, and all he is asking from us is a place for his people to worship God without interference. Guido Vasquez and I met last week about this very thing, and we had enough flyers printed and delivered to reach every citizen, threatening severe penalties for violations of the ordinance. Mr. Shepherd told me that if his people can't freely worship, then he is going to close up the factory and return all his people to Tennessee, where they live, and we certainly don't want that to happen. We not only don't want it to happen, San Sorento can't afford for it to happen.

"Tomas, what do you think your police force can do? Do you know any of the people involved In the First Born of the Lamb group?"

"Yes sir, over the years, we have had encounters with several of them."

The president said, "Well, here's the first thing I want you to do. As soon as you leave here, I want you to go back to your office and put together the names of every member of the FBL that you have had trouble with in the past, and then, in the morning, I want all the officers that is necessary from your department to go in person to their home or workplace and get across to them what's going to happen, not only to them, personally, but to San Sorento if these threats or warnings persist. We only have one more week to correct the situation. Now, Mr. Shepherd's group is supposed to meet here, in this building, Sunday morning, and I want you to post armed guards here before and during their meeting. Mr. Shepherd, do you have anything else that you want to say?"

"Only this, Mr. President. I appreciate your efforts in trying to contain the suppression we have encountered, and I appreciate your order for armed guards before and during our meeting, Sunday, however, I would hope that the guards will be in plain clothes and not in uniforms. Would that be possible?"

"Not only will it be possible, but I was going to tell Chief Morin to do that before you mentioned it. Anything else?"

"Yes. I would like to invite you and your aide and you, Chief Marin and Captain Gonzalez to attend our worship service, Sunday morning. You can learn, firsthand, about the God we worship, and who knows, you may want to start worshipping Him, yourselves."

President Putra said, "Thank you so much for inviting me. I'm going to tell my wife about this, so don't be surprised if you see us. I've heard about this religion all my life, but I've never had an opportunity to witness it, personally. I'll look forward to meeting with you and your people."

Chief Marin said, "I'm not sure I can be there, but I appreciate your invitation. I'll talk to my wife about it, and if she would like to come, we'll be there."

President Putra told his aide that when they got back to their office, to have someone come down here and clean up the mess, the arsonist left.

When they finished, and President Putra had left to go back to his office, Monty left to go to the plant. He wanted to talk to Bill Glasser about the upcoming Sunday service. Joan went with him, and when they got there, she stayed with Bimo while Monty went back to the cutting department to see Bill.

"Good morning, Boss," Bill said when he saw him.

"Good morning, Bill. How are you doing?"

"I'm fine. Have you checked to see if they took the chairs to the building yet?"

"Yesh, I just left there, and that's why I'm here. The chairs are taken care of, and when I went by to check on them, somebody had burned a fire on the walkway leading up to the front door. I called President Putra and told him about it, and not only he, but his aide and the Chief of Police and a Police Captain came out there to see what was going on. The Police chief said he thought it was a warning from the First Born of the Lamb or the FBL to scare us off from having our church services there."

"What are we going to do, Monty?"

"We're going to have church the way we planned.

President Putra ordered the Police Chief to go back to his office and compile a list of everybody in the FBL they had ever had a problem with, and to send an officer to see every one of them and explain what would happen to them if they were to attempt to disrupt any of our meetings."

Bill asked, "Do you think that will help?"

"I do. Between flyers delivered to every citizen and personal visits by the police officers, I think church should be safe. As a matter of fact, President Putra said he and his wife are coming to our meeting Sunday."

"Are you serious?"

"I'm very serious."

"Monty, are you going to be there?"

"Yeah. I was planning to go home, but with this latest threat, I'm going to stay, at least until our plane goes back next week."

"Monty, can I ask a favor?"

"Sure. What is it?"

"Well, I know I told you that I would lead the devotions at our Sunday meetings, but Monty, I never dreamed the president would be at any of our meetings. I don't have a command of the English language the way you do. It's especially not good enough to try to teach a president. Would you consider leading the devotion for me Sunday?"

"Bill, you probably have a better command of the English language than I do, and I understand that you know the Bible really well. Let me tell you something. When you teach someone anything; whether it be the Bible or something else, it means you know more about what you're teaching than they do, whether it be a president or a janitor. Whether you're a good orator or not makes no difference. All that matters is if you're able to get your point across to your student. I'm ninety-nine and three quarters percent sure that you know a whole lot more than President Putra does about the Bible, and you would do well teaching him, but if it will make you feel better, I'll lead the service, Sunday, but Bill, I probably won't be here for any more, after Sunday."

"I understand. Thanks, Boss."

They talked for a couple more minutes, and then Monty went up to Bimo's office to get Joan. On the way to the car, he asked, "Would you like to have a cheeseburger?"

"I'd love to have a cheeseburger."

"How about we go to the Pueblo Grill?"

"Suits me. Let's go."

After lunch, they went back to the hotel and got ready for a good afternoon at the beach. They only had a few days left, so they wanted to take advantage of the good weather and ultimately go back to Chattanooga and show off their tans.

Sofia and Bimo hadn't been seeing each other too much on work nights. Sofia's duties, training new bottom hemmers as well as running a sewing machine, herself, really took it out of her, and she wanted to rest when she got to the Dunes after work every day, but they both looked forward to Friday nights because they didn't have to get up and go to work on Saturday. She was tired on Friday night as well, but thinking ahead to not having to work the next day seemed to give her energy.

Bimo took her to the Dunes after work, and they decided to do something different that night. He gave her a choice between going to a club and dancing the Salsa most of the night or going on a Taco Tour. He said they could do one, one night and the other the next night. She thought about the choices he gave her, and after a couple of minutes, she said, "Why don't we do the Salsa thing tonight? I'm afraid that if I do that tomorrow night, I might not want to go to church on Sunday. If we do the Taco Tour tomorrow night, then I can stop whenever I want to and still feel good when I get ready for church, Sunday."

"Okay then. Salsa it is. Club Morales doesn't open until eight or nine o'clock, so if we wait until then to eat, we're going to be starved. Why don't you eat some cheese crackers or something light to tide you over until you get to the club. Have you ever done the Salsa before?"

"Oh yeah. There is a Mexican club in Chattanooga, and my friend and I go there some, and they do the Salsa there. It's a lot of fun. I'm looking forward to going tonight."

He picked her up at eight thirty, and they headed to Club Morales. They had only just opened, and there weren't many people there yet, so they took advantage of the slow period to order and eat some food. They stayed until a little after midnight and got plenty of exercise when they did the Salsa, which was about every other dance.

Bimo took her back to the Dunes when they left Club Morales, and they sat in the Explorer for a while, before she got out, and smooched. When she finally opened the door to get out, she told Bimo how much fun she had had and said she would love to do that again sometime.

He said, "I'd like to, too. Maybe we can do it again next week. I enjoyed tonight. I'll see you tomorrow."

Sunday morning.

The Tour bus was sitting at the Dunes at nine fifteen, and it began to fill up about twenty after, and by nine thirty, it was full. Alvaro, the driver, asked Bill if he should take the ones on the bus to the church building and come back after the others, and Bill said he thought he could get the overage in his van, and when Bimo got there in the Explorer, that would add a couple more places, so he didn't think it would be necessary for him to bring the bus back again.

Monty drove by in his Suburban, just in case there were some that needed a ride. When he saw that the bus stop was empty, he went on to the church. Bimo and Sofia were going in at the same time as Monty and Joan, and Monty asked Bimo if he would make a count of the number of people attending. Just as they were getting ready to shut the door, several people looked toward the door, and President and Mrs. Putra were coming in. Bimo took it upon himself to usher them as close to the front as he could, where they could maybe hear better.

After Bimo seated President and Mrs. Putra, he went back and closed the door, and then took his seat next to Sofia.

At that point, Monty stood up and told everyone how glad he was to see them, and that he was especially glad to see President and Mrs. Putra. There were also some present that were brought by the Chattanooga workers, who couldn't speak English, and Champak interpreted the way she did the previous Sunday.

He said, "I was raised in church and ever since I can remember, we had music before the spoken word, and this morning, I would like for us to have a song, even though we don't have any song books to go by, but I think you folks from Chattanooga probably all know Jesus Loves Me and can sing it without music. You folks from San Sorento may not know who we will be singing about, but He's the one I'll be talking about today. I'm no singer, but I'm going to attempt to lead you in the song," and he stopped talking and began to sing Jesus Loves Me. Most of the Chattanooga people joined in, and without song books, they didn't know the words to any other verses except the first one, so they quit singing after that one.

Monty began to speak, and the Scriptures he chose were the first chapter of Genesis and the fourteenth chapter of John, verse six. Since several of the people there had heard the name God, they didn't really know who He is, and it was doubtful if any of them, other than the Chattanoogans had even heard the name Jesus, so he tried his best to make it simple for them to understand.

He started by reading Genesis one, where it says in the beginning, God created Heaven and Earth. He realized he didn't have a whole lot of time, so he tried to cover as much of the Old Testament as he could, and still have time to get into the New Testament.

When he got to the New Testament, he concentrated on how God sent his Son, Jesus, to Earth to be killed and then come back to life in three days in order to save all of us from our sins. He told them how, if they would accept Jesus into their hearts, they would go and be with Him when they died.

Monty had a way about him that made people want to listen to him. He spoke with authority, and whatever he said, people believed. At the end of his message that morning, he issued an invitation to anybody there that wished to be saved from their sins, to come down to where he was standing, and they would have prayer, and that would be a sign to others that they had accepted Jesus and were saved. Instead of an invitation hymn like one who was used to going to church would expect he began the song Jesus Loves Me and used that as the invitation.

He was gratified as well as surprised by some who came forward to accept Christ. First, there were three women from Chattanooga and three San Sorento women, and then, as a huge and grateful surprise, both President and Mrs. Putra accepted Jesus.

Monty almost choked up when the president came down, and he thanked God for it. President Putra also had moisture in his eyes, and he thanked Monty profusely for allowing him the chance to come into his group and hear about Christ. He assured him that he was going to use whatever influence he had to try and spread the word to his entire country.

After the welcome to the eight who came forward, Monty led them in prayer, thanking God for all his blessings and the ones who accepted Christ that morning, and he asked God to please help all of them to be faithful witnesses for Him. When he finished his prayer and before he broke up into informal conversations, he told the people there, that he was going to call his office, the next morning, and have Jimmy send a supply of Bibles and songbooks, in both English and Spanish, and he hoped they would be there on the next plane.

Early the next morning, Monty called Jimmy. "Good morning, Son."

"Hi Dad. What's up this morning?"

"There are two or three things I need for you to do, and I'd like for you to do them before the next plane leaves to come out here, if you can."

"What are they, Dad?"

"First of all, I want you to call the Bible bookstore there in town and order a hundred and twenty-five

Living Bibles. If they have them in Spanish, get fifty in English and seventy-five in Spanish. Also, if they have hymnals, get a hundred and twenty-five of them; fifty in English and seventy five in Spanish and if you can, send them over here on the next plane.

"Now, let me tell you what happened in church yesterday. We had fifty of our people there and fourteen San Sorentoans. After I gave the invitation, eight people came down. Three Chattanoogans and five San Sorentoans and guess who two of the San Sorentoans were."

"Was Bimo one of them?"

"No. Bimo made a decision last Sunday. The two I'm talking about are none other than President and Mrs. Putra."

"You're kidding. President and Mrs. Putra?"

"No, I'm not kidding, and do you know what president Putra told me?"

"What?"

"He said he is going to use whatever influence he has to try and spread the word of Jesus throughout his whole country, and that made me think about getting a Missionary over here. How about calling our preacher and ask him how do we go about finding an 'on fire' Missionary, and oh yeah, I have an account with the Bible bookstore. Tell them to charge the Bibles and song books to me."

"Okay, Dad. I'll take care of it. When are you and Mom coming home?"

"If nothing happens, we'll be home on the next

plane. When will that be? Do you know?"

"As you know, it was there over the weekend, so it will be next Saturday or Sunday."

"Oh Jimmy, while I'm thinking about it, see if the bookstore has any good daily devotion books in Spanish, and if they do, send about a hundred of them; fifty in each language."

He and Jimmy talked about some Shepherd Apparel business for a while after he told Jimmy what he wanted concerning the church in San Sorento, and then he hung up. Joan was up and dressed by that time, so they went downstairs for breakfast.

After they returned to their room, his phone rang. Without looking at the ID, he answered it, and the voice on the other end said, "Good morning, Monty. This is Arin Putra. How are you this morning?"

"Good morning, Arin. I'm fine, thank you."

"Monty. Juanita and I enjoyed the service yesterday, and we want to thank you for leading us to Jesus. We have several questions, however, and we'd both like to talk to you. Do you think you and your wife could come to our house for dinner this evening?"

"Yes sir. It would be our pleasure. I will need directions, though."

"You won't have to worry about that. I'll send a car for you. To give us plenty of time to talk, will five o'clock work for you?"

"Five o'clock will work just fine."

"Good. We'll look forward to seeing you then."

"Thank you, Arin."

Chapter Twelve

He turned to Joan and said, "Well, Miss High Class. It seems that you've arrived."

"What do you mean?"

"You've just been invited to the President of San Sorento's home for dinner tonight. Do you think you can clear your calendar to make it, or should I call them and tell them that you're just too busy?"

She couldn't help but smile, and she said, "Don't call them. I'll cancel something else in order to go. It's really hard being so popular."

"I'm sure it is. Just try to hold yourself down tonight when you're talking to the president and his wife."

"I'll try."

Being serious, she asked Monty, "What will I wear to the president's house. Do I have to really dress up?"

"I don't think so. Just wear something a little better than what you wear to the beach. Pretend we're going to a nice restaurant. I'm not going to wear a tie, but I may wear a sport coat. I'm sure they'll make us feel at home."

At five o'clock they were waiting in the lobby when the president's car arrived. The driver came in and spotted them right away and told them who he was. He led them outside to a very nice Mercedes and drove them to an opulent neighborhood that neither Monty or Joan had seen before. The Putra's house sat on a beautiful two or three-acre lot with an attractive fence surrounding the entire property. It was secured by an electronic gate, which the driver activated with a remote in the car.

As they were waiting on the driver to come around and open their door, Joan asked, "What do you think they'll have to eat?"

"I don't know. It probably won't be a chimichanga or burritos. It will probably be something fancy. Pretend you like it, even if you don't."

The chauffer's name was Onkar Medina, and when they got to the president's house, they found out that Onkar also acted as the butler. He opened the front door for them, and when they got inside, he said, "Please wait here and I'll get the president."

In a few seconds, President Putra and his wife, Juanita, came into the foyer and greeted them.

He said, "Hi, Monty, Hi, Joan. I'm glad you could come. Let's go into the drawing room and sit down. Juanita and I have some questions we want to ask you."

As they walked to the drawing room, Joan said, "You sure have a lovely home," and Juanita said, "Thank you."

Just as they were getting ready to go into the drawing room, a very handsome young man, and beautiful young lady came up to them, and President

Putra said, "Monty, Joan, I'd like for you to meet our son, Arin, and our daughter Mariana. Arin, Mariana, this is Mr. and Mrs. Monty Shepherd. Mr. and Mrs. Shepherd are from Chattanooga, Tennessee, in the United States."

Both kids said what sounded like the same thing, and Monty and Joan took it to mean, "We're glad to meet you," and Joan and Monty said, "We're glad to meet you, too."

President Putra asked Monty, "Would you mind if my children sat in on our conversation? I'd like for them to hear your answers to my questions because I hope to be able to lead them to Christ the way you did me. Just talk normally. They have been studying English, and they might be able to understand you even better than I can."

"Of course, I don't mind. I would love to be able to share the Word of God to the whole world. Come in, Arin and Mariana. I hope you will like what you hear. Would you like for Onkar to sit in on it, too?"

"Yes," and he told Arin to go get Onkar and ask him to come in there."

When Onkar got there, President Putra asked, "Onkar, Monty is going to explain what he told us in church, yesterday. Would you like to hear it?" And Onkar said he would.

After they were seated, Monty said, "Arin, you said that you and Juanita have some questions about what you heard yesterday. Is there something in particular that you want to know?"

"The whole thing was sort of confusing, and if you have the time, we wish you would kind of summarize everything you said, especially the part about Jesus getting killed and then rising from the dead to save our souls."

"Okay. First, do you both understand that God created everything, including you and me?"

"Yes, we understand that. We want to hear more about Jesus. Can you tell us about Him being born of a virgin and then coming forward?"

"Sure, I can," and he began with Mary's conception and brought the story of Jesus forward to his crucifixion and resurrection."

He talked for an hour or longer, and he was interrupted several times by all four of the Putras, and when he was through, he asked, "Do you think you understand better today than you did yesterday?"

Arin said, "I do. Do you, Juanita?" and she said she did.

Monty said, "Don't worry if you don't understand everything. I've been worshipping God my whole life and I've studied the Bible for most of my life, and I still don't understand it all. You don't have to understand it all. All you have to do is believe that Jesus died and rose again and by doing that, he saved us from our sins if we ask Him to come into our hearts."

As they were winding up the conversation, a lady dressed in a white smock came to the door and said, "Mr. and Mrs. Putra, dinner is served," and they all got up and went into a huge dining room, where there was a table that seated fourteen people. Since there were only six of them, they only used about half of it. President Putra said, "Monty, Joan, I don't know if you've ever had what we're having tonight, and I hope you enjoy it. It's one of our favorites."

Monty said, "I'm sure we'll like it. We like most everything."

Just then the lady in the white smock pushed a cart in, loaded with some kind of shrimp dish for the appetizer. Joan took a bite and said, "This is absolutely out of this world. I know it's shrimp, but I don't know what kind. What is this, Juanita?"

She answered, "It's just a simple cilantro lime shrimp. I'm glad you like it."

After the appetizer, the lady pushed in another cart loaded with food, and Monty said, "Boy, this looks delicious."

The lady served the president and Monty first, then the ladies, and finally, the children.

When Joan started eating, she said, "This is so good. I'm not sure what it is. Is this something I can fix at home?"

Juanita said, "I'm sure you can. It's called Chipotle Mexican Risotto, and you can buy the ingredients almost anywhere."

"Well I'm sure going to try it."

Before they got to dessert, the phone rang, and in just a minute, Onkar opened the door and said, "Mr. President, you have a phone call. It's Tomar Marin, and he says it's important."

The president excused himself and left the room to get the phone somewhere else. In about five minutes, he came back into the dining room and said, "Monty that was terrible news. That was Tomas Marin, our Chief of Police. You remember him, don't you?"

"Yes. I remember him."

"Tomas called to tell me that your church building is on fire. The Fire Department is there, but it doesn't look good for saving the building. Do you want to go with me to the building?"

"Yes, if you don't mind."

"Do you mind if Joan stays here with Juanita?"

"Is that alright with you, Honey?"

She said it was, so Arin, Monty, and Onkar jumped in the car and rushed to the scene of the fire with the flashers on the Mercedes telling people they were in a hurry. When they got near, they saw lights flashing everywhere. When the guards holding the public back saw that it was the president, they waved them in, and Onkar drove up as close as he could without interfering with the firemen. There were three fire trucks and no telling how many firemen fighting the blaze, which to an average person would think was out of control.

The fire Chief came over to talk to the president, and when President Putra asked what started the fire, the chief said he didn't know. They would have to wait until after the fire was out before they could investigate.

Monty said, "I think I know. I hope I'm wrong, but I'm pretty sure I know what started it." The president and police chief both just looked at him without saying anything, and he told them, "And I'll bet you all know what started it, too." Silence.

After so long a time, the fire was brought under control, but not until it had almost totally destroyed the building.

The police chief instructed some of his men to put up tapes like crime scene tape, and for two of them to remain there all night just in case someone who had something to do with the fire came back for some reason."

Monty and the president remained there for quite a while before returning to the president's house to pick up Joan. Arin told Monty on the way to his house, "I don't know what to say, Monty. I was confident that after our flyers were delivered, the people still involved with the FBL cult would come to their senses and accept the fact that the FBL is no longer in existence.

"You don't need to say anything, Arin. I know it's not your fault, but I also know we still have a problem."

Arin said, "I hope this doesn't mean what I think it means. Do you think we can talk in the morning?"

Monty said, "I think we have to talk. Give me a time and I'll be there. Where are we going to talk? At your office?"

"Yes. That will be the best place."

They rode the rest of the way to Arin's house in total silence. As they were pulling into the driveway, Arin asked, "Can I ask what you're thinking, Monty?"

Monty said, "You don't want to know. I know what I would like to do, but since I've involved God in this, I'm not going to make a decision until I pray about it and ask God what he wants me to do. Now that you know God, yourself, I suggest that you pray, also. If we both do this, then I think we'll probably come to the right outcome."

"Monty, can I tell you something?"

"Yeah. What?"

"Monty, I don't know if I know how to pray or not."

"Just talk to God like you're talking to another person. Just keep in mind that He is the ultimate authority over everything, and whatever He tells you to do is always right. You might not like His answer, but it's always right. He's probably not going to come out and speak to you in an actual voice, but if you're serious when you pray, you'll get a certain feeling, and you'll know what He is saying."

"Okay. I'll try."

Onkar was standing outside the car while they talked and he sensed when they were through, and he opened the door for them. Monty got out with Arin because he wanted to go in for a second and tell Juanita how much he enjoyed dinner. As he was leaving, he turned around and said, "Arin, please tell

Arin and Mariana how much I enjoyed meeting them, and that I'm sorry I had to run out on them. Thank you again for dinner, Juanita,"

He and Joan went to the car, and Onkar took them back to the hotel. On the way, Monty asked him several questions about himself and working for President Putra, but he stayed away from talking about the fire.

In a few minutes they pulled up to the hotel entrance, and Onkar opened his door, and before he could get out, Monty said, "Keep seated, Onkar. We can open our door and get out, but thank you, anyway. Do you have to go back to the president's house tonight?"

"Si."

"Well, I'm sorry we kept you out so late, tonight."

"Thank you, sir. It's no problem. I enjoyed meeting you and Mrs. Shepherd, and I hope to see you again."

"Thank you, Onkar. Good night."

He and Joan went straight upstairs after they arrived at the hotel, and both of them just collapsed into the easy chairs in their room. The long day and the stress of actually going to the president's house and having dinner with him and his family and then the stress of the fire had drained them, both mentally and physically.

Joan asked, "Honey, what do you think you're going to do?"

"I really don't know. If this was a week and a half

ago, I know what I would have done, but now, I'm not sure. I've got some praying to do tonight, and hopefully, I can get an answer."

She asked, "What's the difference in a week and a half ago and this week?"

"Well a week and a half ago, all we seemed to have were problems, and I was ready to pull out, but then, last Sunday, Bimo accepted Christ, and then yesterday, Arin and Juanita Putra along with three other folks from San Sorento and three of our own people from Chattanooga accepted Him, and that's nine souls out of just a handful of people. Now, if nine people are saved out of only about fifty or sixty and only by hearing God's word once or twice, what can happen if we can reach hundreds over here, and the saved can overrule the PBL cult and make this country into a Christian nation. Don't you think I'd be sorry if I closed the plant and took everything away from these people and they didn't have another chance to meet Jesus. Most importantly, I think God would be sorry if I do that. Don't you?"

"I think He would, but let me ask you this, Darling. You're spending so much time over here, now, are you going to have to just stay over here for a long period of time or are you going to be able to come home some?"

"I'm coming home, but with things happening the way they are over here right now, I don't see how I can leave. I was planning on going home on the plane leaving today or tomorrow until the fire, and now I have to stay and try to make some sense out of things. I hope they will catch whoever set the fire and we can sort of relax, but as long as somebody's out there wanting to burn us out or even kill us, it looks as if I'm here for a while longer. I'm going to meet with Arin at his office in the morning, and maybe we can get things worked out. There's nothing I'd like better. Now, Honey, if you want to leave for Chattanooga on the next plane, you certainly can, and if you want to stay here with me, you can certainly do that, too. It's your call."

"I'll think about it. I'm tired, and right now, I'm going to bed. Are you coming?"

"Not right now. I won't be long."

She went on to bed, but Monty stayed up for a little while. He wanted to pray before he went to bed in hopes that he would be given an idea of what to do overnight.

Chapter Thirteen

While Joan and Monty were in the hotel dining room, the next morning, Monty's phone rang, and it was President Putra. "Good morning, Monty. Did you sleep well last night?"

"As a matter of fact, I did. I turned everything over to Jesus to handle, and I slept like a log. Did you sleep well?"

"Surprisingly so, I did. Listen. About our meeting this morning, never mind about driving over here. I'm going to send Onkar to get you, and he should be there at five after ten. I've already told Chief Marin to be here, and I think I'll call Guido Vasquez to come sit in. Maybe, between the four of us, we can get something worked out. Is that alright with you?"

"It is. The more, the merrier."

"Very well. I'll look forward to seeing you at ten thirty. Goodbye."

Onkar was right on time at five after ten. Monty hurried out to the car because he didn't want Onkar to get out and come around to open the door for him, but he was too slow. Onkar beat him to it.

"Good morning, Mr. Shepherd. It's nice to see you, this morning."

"Thank you, Onkar. It's nice to see you, too."

"Are you ready for a big day, Mr. Shepherd?"

"I hope so, Onkar, but I have found that in San

Sorento, you never know what's going to happen from one minute to the next."

In the meantime, word was out about the fire at the Shepherd Church the night before, and Bimo, especially, was worried about it because he knew what Monty had already said about closing the plant and taking all his people home. His feelings for Sofia had become very strong, and he was petrified at the thought of losing her if the plant closed. At the morning break, he talked to her about what they would do if Monty closed the plant. Her feelings for him had become very strong, also, and she didn't know the answer.

She asked, "Do you really think he'll shut the plant down?"

"I wouldn't be surprised. His convictions are so strong that he's not going to do anything to jeopardize what he thinks is right. Besides, he can afford to do whatever he wants to. I know he has spent a lot of money on this deal, but that's not as important to him as his relationship with the Lord. All I can say right now is be prepared. If we have any ideas about a future together, we need to make plans now."

"Do you think we have a future together?" she asked.

"I'd like to think so. Have you thought about that at all?"

"I have, but I dismiss it because I don't see how it could possibly work, since you live here and I live in America. If the plant closes, I don't see how I could stay over here because there aren't that many jobs available, and I don't think you would want to move to America since this is your home. Would you?"

"I might. I don't know anything but clothing manufacturing, and I'd have to get a job doing that, but maybe Monty would hire me over there. He knows that I know what I'm doing when it comes to running a garment plant. Are we going to see each other tonight?"

"If you want to, and if I'm not too tired."

"Okay, we'll talk more about it tonight."

Onkar parked in the place reserved for the president's car when they got to the Capitol, and Monty said, "I've got my door, Onkar, but thank you anyway." Onkar walked around the car, and they walked into the Capitol together; Monty to the president's office and Onkar somewhere else.

When he got to the president's office, President Putra was waiting on him and the Police Chief was already there. The president asked Monty, "Guido Vasquez should be here any minute. Would you like a cup of coffee while we wait?"

"Yes. Thank you," and Rosa Matzos, his secretary and assistant brought coffee for the three of them. While they waited on Guido, they couldn't help but talk about the fire the night before, and in about ten minutes, Guido came in and apologized for being tardy.

President Putra said, "I'm glad you're here, Guido. As you know by now, the building where

Monty was holding church services burned last night, and it's urgent that we not only find who did it, but also stop it from happening in the future. We all know what Mr. Shepherd said he was going to do before we met and decided on the flyers, and apparently the flyers haven't worked, so we're just praying and hoping he doesn't decide to close the clothing plant. The purpose of this meeting this morning is to try and figure out a way to stop the FBL cult from influencing the evil it has created for the past several years, and to let Mr. Shepherd see that we are truly trying to work with him in hopes that he will continue to work with us."

Monty already knew what he was going to do, but he wanted to hear from the three officials, and what they were prepared to do before he said anything.

President Putra said, "Guido, do you think the Legislature would be open to me letting the Shepherd Church services meet here at the Capitol, temporarily? I feel that they would be safe here, and we need to ensure their safety. What do you think?"

"I think that's a good idea, Mr. President. I'll have to bring it before the whole body, but from what I have heard different ones say, the majority will want to go along with it. I suggest you go ahead and plan to have them here until and unless you hear differently from me."

"Okay. Thank you, Guido. Now, number two. Tomas, what are you going to do to catch whoever burned the church?"

"Mr. President, I had an early meeting with some of my key people before I came here, and it was decided that the first thing we're going to do is to revisit the FBL members that we questioned a week or two ago. We feel that one or more of them are the most likely to have set the fire. We'll try to determine who among those are the most dedicated, and we'll question them first. If we find that none of those are guilty, then we have additional lists of FBL members that we'll question. Other than cult members, we have no idea who might be against other religions."

The Police Chief and President talked at length about who they might start with, and they narrowed down the first half dozen in hopes the guilty party would be one of them. They had a pretty long list, so if the arsonist wasn't in the first half dozen, it might take a long time to find the guilty one.

When the two of them finished their discussion, President Putra looked over at Monty and said, "Okay, Mr. Shepherd. I guess the floor is yours. Dare I ask what you plan to do, now that your church has been burned."

"Mr. President, if you had asked me that a week and a half ago, my answer would have been different, but it seems as though God has been working in San Sorento, and I feel that I need to do what I think He has told me to do, rather than what I would choose to do. Before I left to come here this morning, my wife asked me the same thing, and this is what I told her.

"I told her that in the last week and a half, nine

souls have been saved here in San Sorento out of no more than sixty people. From what I hear, there are quite a few people wanting to hear God's Word, and if I shut down and leave without sharing His Word, then I will be the one to blame for letting those people down. What if we can get a hundred or even two hundred in church next Sunday to hear God's Word? How many of those will be saved? Then, if those go out to their friends and families and tell them about the Word and get them to come to church and on and on, this could be the beginning of changing San Sorento from evil FBL cult followers into a Christian Nation, and I firmly believe that God will reward us for being a part of it. Mr. President, if you and your wife will share your newfound faith with others, I'm sure you will be richly blessed.

"Now, I've said a lot to say this. No, as long as there are people here who want to change for the better, I won't close Shepherd Apparel/San Sorento. Now that I've said that, let's catch that arsonist."

President Putra, all smiles, said, "Thank you, Monty. As far as I'm concerned, you're a great man, and the people of San Sorento thank you, also. Well, gentlemen, we now have our answer, so let's get started making San Sorento a better place to live and work. This meeting is adjourned. Thank you for being here."

Of course, the end of the formal meeting didn't mean that the attendees were going to leave. They stood around and drank coffee until almost lunchtime, and talked about what they were going to do from each of their positions to help improve San Sorento.

Finally, Chief Marin left, and then Representative Vasquez left after telling Monty how much he appreciated what he was doing for his country. As he was leaving, he turned and told Monty, "My wife and I will see you Sunday morning."

Monty replied, "Good. Bring your friends."

After he left, President Putra asked Monty, "Can I buy your lunch?"

"Thank you, sir. That would be nice."

The president said, "We have our own cafeteria here, if that's alright."

"That's perfect", Monty said.

They went to the cafeteria, and instead of talking about arson, or God or anything else having to do with what was going on, President Putra talked about his children, and how he sometimes felt that his position was holding them back. He knew that Monty had children and was basically in the same place as he was, except Monty's position was not in politics. He hoped that Monty could give him some firsthand experiences that would help him, and Monty was glad to share his children's lives with him.

After lunch Arin had Onkar take Monty back to his hotel and Joan. Before he went upstairs, he checked by the pool because he had a hunch she would be out there, and sure enough, she was laid back on a chaise lounge reading a book, written by her favorite author, Bud Fussell. He walked up to her and asked, "Hi, Sugar Plum. What's cooking?"

"Nothing, really. I'm just getting into this book, and I can hardly wait to get to the end."

"Well, I told the powers to be in San Sorento that I would not shut down the clothing mill, and they are happy. Honey, it looks as if I'm going to have to be here at least one more week before I can go home, and I'd like for you to stay with me, but if you feel that you need to go home, I'll put you on the plane that will be leaving Thursday."

"Darling, I want to stay with you. I've never left you on your own in the past, and I don't intend to now."

"Atta girl. I love you. Do you know that? Listen, I'm going to go down to the plant for a little bit. I need to see Bill Glasser and Bimo. Do you want to go?"

"If you don't mind, I think I'll stay here and nurse this book."

"That's fine. Maybe we can go out and celebrate my decision tonight."

He left and went to the plant, and everything seemed to be running smoothly. He spoke to the office ladies as he went through and headed back to the cutting department. At first, he didn't see Bill, but then he spotted him at another cutting table showing one of the new cutters how to do something. He waited until he finished with the new man, and then he motioned for him to come over to where he was.

"Hi Boss," Bill said.

"Hi. Is your new cutter working out?"

"Yes sir. He's going to be a good one."

"Bill, I want to talk to you for a minute. First, I think I owe you an apology. I asked you to lead the Sunday services and instead of letting you do what I asked, I've taken over, and I'm sorry, but I have felt that under the circumstances, it was necessary."

"Boss, you don't owe me an apology. If anybody owes anybody anything, I owe you a 'thank you' for not leaving me in such a mess as we've had with the cult."

"Bill, after talking to the president and other state officials, and after much prayer, I've decided not to close the plant, but to keep it open and remain in San Sorento, at least for the time being. The government has told me that we can hold services at the Capitol until the arsonist is caught and things die down. My main reason for deciding this is because we've had nine decisions for the Lord made out of about sixty people, and I reasoned that if we could continue to add people each week, and if they would tell others, then there's no telling what might happen on this island. At any rate, I don't want to be the one to stop everything and leave the unsaved hanging, at least until they've had a chance to hear the Gospel.

"Having said that, I came to tell you that I'm going to stay here for at least one more week, and I think there are going to be some people there Sunday that I would like to talk to personally, so if you don't mind,

I'll handle things again, this coming Sunday."

"I don't mind, Boss. I'd love for you to do it every Sunday. You're such a better speaker than I am, when you speak you speak with authority, and the people believe what you say."

"Okay, Buddy. I'll see you Sunday, if not before."

"See ya, Boss. Thank you."

When he left Bill, he went out into the sewing department to see Bimo. He saw him right away, and he was talking to Luiz Garza, the man he was training to be the plant manager. He walked up to them and said, "Hi, Guys."

Bimo responded with, "Hi Monty. How ya doing?" and Luiz didn't say anything. Monty said, "What are you guys doing, solving the world's problems?"

Bimo said, "We were just talking about the church being burned last night and wondering who set it. I sure hope they catch whoever did it real quick. We don't need that kind of stuff going on."

Monty said, "Maybe they will. I know they're working hard on it," and Luiz said, "I doubt they'll ever catch them."

His statement bothered Monty. He thought to himself, *this guy said, catch them and not catch him, which is what everybody is saying. Very interesting.* He filed the remark in the back of his mind and continued talking to them. He said, "Bimo, I know you've been worried that I was going to close this place, but as of now, I'm not going to close it."

"Wow. What happened to change your mind?"

"As you know, I was upset that we had no place for our people to worship, and everybody seemed to be afraid of the FBL cult, and the feeling is that the cult burned us out. Well, as of this morning, we have been given a nice, large, and above all, a safe place to hold our services, and now, since our people can freely worship, there's no need to close the plant."

"Where is this place, Monty?"

"Would you believe in the San Sorento Capitol building?"

"That's great. I know it was very nice when we were there a week ago. Will this be every week?"

"Yeah." The whole time he was telling this to Bimo, an unimaginable look was on Luiz' face. Then he said, "This is great news, isn't it Guys?"

"It sure is," Bimo said.

Monty said, "Luiz, don't you think this is great news?" and Luiz just muttered something in Spanish that he could not understand. The terrible look was still on his face. He stored all of this in his mind and told them he had to go, and left.

Meanwhile, at Police Headquarters, Chief Marin was in a meeting with the two detectives he had chosen to head up the team to hopefully arrest the church arsonist. Their names were Berto Ochoa, who would be the lead detective and Dario Barrero. They were both long time veteran detectives who Chief Marin thought would be the best to handle the investigation because they had both worked on cases involving the FBL in the past.

Berto asked Dario, "We've got a pretty good list of suspects. Which one do you want to start with?"

"I'd say, Alfredo Diaz. There's just something about that guy that I don't trust. I've had run ins with him before."

"Alfredo it is. Let's go see him."

Chapter Fourteen

They drove down into what looked to be the low end of town to what some people would call a shack. There were two old cars and several toys lying around the yard. Berto pushed the doorbell button, but didn't hear any doorbell, so he knocked loudly on the door with his hand. After a few minutes, a character came to the door, and Dario said, "Hi Alfredo."

Alfredo asked, "What do you want?"

Dario replied, "I haven't seen you in a while, Alfredo. How have you been?"

Again, Alfredo asked, "What do you guys want?"

Then Berto said, "I guess by now you have heard that the church building used by the Shepherd people was burned down last night, haven't you?"

"No, I don't know anything about any building being burned down. Why are you here?"

"Alfredo, it's common knowledge that members of the Church of the First Born of the Lamb of God have threatened and terrorized members of other religions, and we know that in the past, you have been one of the terrorists. Where were you last night?"

"I was at work."

"What hours were you at work?"

"From three o'clock to eleven o'clock."

"Where do you work, Alfredo?"

"At the Surfside Hotel."

"What do you do there?"

"I work second shift maintenance."

"And you were there from three to eleven last night?"

During the whole time of questioning, Dario was taking notes, and when Berto said, "Okay, I guess that's all for now. See you, Alfredo," they went to their car and left. The first thing they did was call the Surfside Hotel and talk to the manager.

"This is detective Berto Ochoa. I'd like some information, please. Do you have an employee working for you named Alfredo Diaz?"

"Yes sir. Alfredo works here. Why? Has he done something wrong?"

"Was he at work yesterday?"

"Hold on and let me check," and in a couple of minutes, he came back to the phone and said, "Yes sir. He was here yesterday. He worked the second shift from three o'clock, yesterday afternoon until eleven o'clock, last night."

"Okay, thank you very much."

"Well, we can mark Alfredo off. His alibi checks out," Berto said. "Do you want to try to see one more today or would you rather get a running start in the morning?"

"Honestly, I would rather go home and get a good start in the morning, but we're pretty close to where Matzo Arroyo lives, so why don't we go by his house and see what he has to say."

"Okay. Sounds good. We'll at least have two

names crossed off the list."

Berto said, "Do you have this guy's address?"

"Yeah," and he gave it to him.

It only took about three or four minutes to get there from Alfredo's. There was no garage, so consequently there was no driveway, so they pulled up out front and walked up a paved walk to the house. Berto rang the doorbell, and while they waited on someone to come, Dario said, "I don't see any cars out front. There might not be anybody home."

Berto rang the bell again, and again they waited, but nobody came to the door, so Berto took out a business card and wrote on it, 'Please call me ASAP,' and stuck it in the door, and they left to go back to headquarters, where they made their plans for the next day.

Monty called Jimmy, just to check in and to tell him that he and his mother were going to stay at least another week. He told him about the fire and the meeting he had with the president and the manhunt. He also told him about the confidence he had that they were going to catch the arsonist and then finding another building for the church He told him to please send another hundred Living Bibles in Spanish.

Jimmy was glad to hear from him, and said the plane was leaving for San Sorento on Thursday, and the first order for Bibles would be on it. He didn't know if he could get the second order on the Thursday plane or not, but he would try.

That evening, as with every other evening, Bimo

and Sofia went out together. That night, they went to the Italiano Restaurante, where there was a nice atmosphere and they could talk in quiet surroundings.

Bimo began the conversation by talking about Monty's decision to keep the plant open, and he said, "Carino, Monty has given us an extension on our relationship by agreeing not to close the plant, but whether it's just going to be just an extension or a permanent situation is going to have to be your decision."

She said, "What do you want it to be?"

He said, "I think you know. I would like for us to be together from now on, but where we would live is a problem. I would hate to leave San Sorento, since it's my lifelong home, and I know you don't want to leave Chattanooga, so what do we do? Monty said in the beginning that the people from Chattanooga might possibly be here for about six months, but the way things are progressing, and the way the new employees are catching on, and the way the older employees are adapting to the Shepherd way, I don't believe you all will be here six months. Already, one month has passed, and knowing what I know about sewing and making clothes, I believe all of you will be taken home in another month or six weeks. That brings me back to what I asked you a few minutes ago. Do you want our relationship to be temporary or do you want it to be permanent?"

"Bebe, you will probably be surprised to know that I have already been thinking about this very thing."

"Have you come up with anything?"

"Maybe. Let me tell you what I thought of. If we get married, I want to get married in Chattanooga, and then, after we're married, we can come here to live, provided we both still have jobs. If we decide that that is something we want to do, before we make any plans, I want to talk to Monty and ask him, after we're married, could I come home on the weekly plane to visit my relatives once every two or three months."

"That's a great idea, Carino. What if Monty says you can only go back once every six months or once a year? Will that kill the deal?"

"I'll have to think about it. I want to be with you, but I also want to see my family more than once or twice a year."

"When are you going to ask him?"

"I don't know. I want to wait until he doesn't have so much on his mind. Right now, he's thinking about the fire and what's going to happen to the church services, because those are the things most important to him. Maybe when they catch whoever burned the church will ease his mind, and I can ask him then."

"What if they haven't caught the guy by the time you're supposed to go home? Are you still not going to ask him?"

"If that happens, then I'll ask him."

"I guess that will have to do, but I hate to have to wait until something may or may not happen to know what I'm going to do with my life."

"Well, Bebe, I'm having to wait, too, but if waiting is too much for you, maybe we should just go our separate ways right now."

"No, no, I'll wait. It's just that it's hard."

"Bimo, let me ask you something. You were born and raised here, and I feel sure you knew or heard about some of the things the FBL did in the past. Do you not or did you not know any of the people connected to the cult? It seems like for such a small place, it would be impossible to not know something about what's going on."

"I knew what was going on when I was a lot younger, but it was my understanding that the FBL disbanded except for a few hard-core members."

"Do you know who those are?"

"I may know them, but even if I know them, I won't know whether they're members of the cult or not."

"Why don't you ask around some and see what you can find out. It could help a lot if you could come up with something. It would help the police or firemen and if there is an arrest, it will help Monty, and if it helps Monty, then it might help you and me. What do you think?"

"You might have something there. Maybe I'll see if I can find out anything. I'll have to be really careful because those people are dangerous. If you cross them, they'll perform what they call 'blood atonement' in a heartbeat. 'Blood atonement' is just another word for murder, but the people who do it try to convince themselves that it's a religious necessity. I may know who one of them is, but I'll have to be very careful if I reveal who he is, because if I do reveal him, he might be able to figure out who squealed on him, and then he and his people would come after me."

"I don't want you to do anything dangerous. The authorities will eventually catch whoever did it."

Bimo asked, "Are you through? If you are, why don't we ride up to the north end of the beach and park for a while?"

"That sounds great. Let's go."

The next morning, Berto and Dario met at Police headquarters and began their day of searching for an arsonist. The day before, they tried to see a man named David Baez, but there was nobody home. Berto left his card on the door, but it was so early, David hadn't called, if he had even planned to call, so the detectives went there first. When they arrived at his house, Berto rang the bell, and after a minute or two, a fairly attractive lady came to the door. Berto and Dario both showed her their badges and asked to see David. The lady said, "He's not here. He's at work. Is there anything I can do for you?"

Without answering her question, Berto asked, "Are you Mrs. Baez?

"Yes, I am."

"What time will he be home?"

She said," It's hard to say. He works on a fishing boat, and if everything is normal, he'll probably be here around five thirty, but if they're lucky enough to catch a large billfish, it might be later. Maybe six thirty or seven. She asked again, "Can I help you with something?"

"No, we just want to ask him a few questions. Does he work those hours every day?"

"Yes. Most days."

"Does he have a regular off day?"

"Usually on Mondays, unless they have a charter."

She asked for the third time. "Is there not anything I can help you with?"

That time, Berto answered, "I'm not sure. You may have heard that a building used for a church was burned the night before last, and we have reason to believe that someone connected to the FBL cult had something to do with burning it. Is your husband a member of the FBL cult?"

"I'm not sure."

"You're not sure if he's a member or not? Most wives would know the answer to a question like that. Are you sure you don't know?"

"Yes, I'm sure I don't know."

Finally, Berto asked her the name of the fishing boat that David worked on, and she said, "Lady Luck."

"Okay, Mrs. Baez, we'll be back in touch."

When they got to their car, Berto asked, "Who's next, Dario?"

"Matzo Arroyo. I've talked to him before."

They drove to a little better neighborhood than the first two. The house had an attached garage, and it looked to be fairly nice. When they got up on the entry level, Berto rang the bell. In a couple of minutes a lady came and Berto asked if this was where Matzo Arroyo lived.

The lady said, "Yes, it is, but he's not here. He's at work."

"Where does he work? Dario asked.

"Over on Isla Fibulon."

"What does he do over there?"

"He's a game warden."

"What time will he be home?"

"Around six o'clock, tonight. Is there anything I can do for you?"

"No ma'am, we just need to talk to him about something. We'll come back. Thank you."

Next, they went to see Aziel Escobar, and he was at work. Then they tried Angel Duran. Same story. At work.

Berto said to Dario, "I can't argue with anybody that has a job, and it looks as if everybody we want to see is working. What do you say to coming back in the evenings to try and see these guys rather than waste our time trying to see them in the daytime when they're working?"

"I'm for that," Dario said.

"Okay. Let's go back to headquarters and run it by the Captain."

They did just that and got the captain's blessings,

and they spent the rest of the day trying to plan exactly what they needed to do to in order to catch the arsonist. After lunch, they took the afternoon off, and decided to meet at headquarters and go back to try and see David Baez.

When they arrived at his house, it was six forty-five, and he was just getting home. When he got out of his car, and before he could get into the house, Berto hollered at him. He stopped and waited for the detectives to get to him, and when they reached him, they showed their badges and introduced themselves.

Berto said, "You must have caught a big one."

"Yeah, one of the men caught a blue marlin that weighed four hundred and seventy pounds, and it took him a while to get it in. What can I do for you fellas?"

Berto said, "David, have you heard about the fire, night before last, that burned the building where they had held religious services?"

"No, I didn't hear anything. Why are you asking me?"

"Because the people who are supposed to know think it was the work of the FBL cult. Are you still a member?"

"Technically I am, but I haven't been active in a long time. In case you're wondering, I didn't have anything to do with it. Like I said, I haven't even heard about it."

Berto asked, "David, how active is the cult right now. Do you have meetings? Do you worship something? What do you do?"

"Like I said, I haven't been active for a long time, so I don't know what the others do."

"David, where were you this past Monday night around seven thirty or eight o'clock?"

"I got home around six o'clock, and I stayed home for the rest of the night. My wife can tell you."

"Would you mind if we ask her, just to verify what you told us?"

"No, I wouldn't mind. I'll call her out here or you can come in."

"If you will, just ask her to come to the door."

He went into the house and in just a minute, both he and his wife came to the door. Berto said, "Hello again, Mrs. Baez. I just need to ask you one question. Where was David from seven thirty or eight o'clock night before last?"

"He was here with me from six o'clock until yesterday morning, when he went to work."

"Okay. Thank you both very much. That's all we have right now. David, if you should hear from any of your FBL buddies and hear anything we need to know. We would very much appreciate it if you would give us a call."

It was still only seven thirty p.m., so they decided to go see Matzo Arroyo. They were surprised to know that he was a game warden, and in their minds, that lent credence to what they thought was going to be the answers to the questions they were going to ask, but they had to ask them, anyway.

As usual, the first thing they did when they met him was to introduce themselves and show their badges.

Matzo said, "It's nice to see you guys. What can I do for you?"

Berto said, "We're investigating the fire that was set the night before last that burned a building where religious services had been held. Have you heard about it?"

"I heard something on the radio about a fire, yesterday, when I was getting ready to go to work That must be the same fire. Why are you asking me about it?"

"Because we have reason to believe that it was set by a person or persons connected to the FBL cult. You're a member of that outfit, aren't you, Matzo?"

He said, "I used to be."

"You used to be? Come on now, Matzo. You still are a member, aren't you?"

"No. Honestly, I'm not."

"Why did you quit?"

"Because they were advocating for things that I wanted no part of."

"Such as?"

"I'd rather not say. Just take my word for it. I'm not a member."

"Where were you night before last, between about six thirty and nine o'clock?""

"I was right here. I got home at six o'clock and stayed here the rest of the night." He looked at his wife and said, "Tell them, Honey."

She said, "he told you right. He was here all night."

"Okay. Thank you very much. That's all for tonight, but we may be back in touch. Good night."

It was not yet eight o'clock, and they wanted to contact at least one more suspect before they quit for the evening, so they went to Angel Duran's because his house was fairly close to the Arroyo's.

When they arrived at the Duran's, Angel and another man were standing outside talking, and when the other man saw who he thought he recognized as detectives, he quickly cut off his conversation with Angel and left in a hurry for his car, brushing against Dario as he went by. Before they got up to Angel, Dario said to Berto, "I think I know that guy."

When they got to Angel, Dario said, "I'm pretty sure I know that guy that just left, but I can't think of his name. What's his name, Angel?"

Angel stood there with a funny look on his face and said, "I don't know who he is. He's just a guy that stopped by to ask directions."

At that point, the detectives showed him their badges and introduced themselves to him.

Angel asked, "What can I do for you fellas tonight?"

Berto said, we're investigating a fire that happened a couple of nights ago, and we hope you can help us."

"A fire? Where?"

"Over on Capo Street. Somebody burned a building down that was being used for religious meetings Have you not heard about it?"

"No. I haven't heard anything about a fire."

Berto asked, "Don't you work over at Gino's Grocery?"

"Yes sir. Why?"

"Because I just can't figure out how somebody who is in touch with that many people every day could not possibly hear about an event as large as that only about a block away."

Looking really strange by now, he said, "I'm sorry. I just haven't heard about it."

"Angel, where were you Monday night from six thirty to nine o'clock?"

"I was here."

"By yourself?"

"Yes sir."

"Did you see anyone else during those hours that can verify your word?"

"No sir."

"How about your wife. Was she not at home?"

"No sir, she had gone over to her sister's, where they watched a movie, and didn't get home until almost midnight."

Berto said, "Okay. That's all for now. Thank you, Angel."

As they were leaving Dario turned and asked, "Angel, are you sure you don't know the name of the man who was here when we got here?"

"I'm sure. I don't know him."

When they got in the car, Berto said, "That guy was lying the whole time we were there."

Dario said, "I feel the same way, and I think that he not only knows that guy's name, I think they're involved with things together."

It was pretty late, so they thought they would wait until the next day to visit anybody else. Since they were going to be working late every night, they waited until late morning to go in to headquarters until they got back to a normal schedule.

The next day, Thursday, the plane arrived from Chattanooga, loaded with fabric, thread, spare sewing machine heads, packaging supplies, and most important to Monty, Bibles.

He was there to meet the plane, and when they unloaded the Bibles, he had them put them in the back of his Suburban.

Berto and Dario arrived at work around eleven fifteen, in time to go to lunch. Before they went, they talked about who they were going to question that day about the fire, and before they got very deep into their plans, Dario told Berto, "I racked my brain last night about that guy we saw at Angel Duran's, and I think I've remembered his name from an FBL crime I helped investigate a while back. He was the ring leader in a 'blood atonement' case that involved a man and his son. You may remember it. I don't know what to think about him being at Angel Duran's unless they're mixed up together on something, and right now, I'd be willing to bet that it's the church fire."

Berto said, "Good work, Dario. You may have just uncovered the answer we're looking for. Let's move him to the top of the list and start looking for him today. Do you have any idea where we can find him? What's his name?"

"I remember in the 'blood atonement' case, when we finally found who performed the deed, the victim's family and others called him *El Diablo*, the devil. He was known by many as *El Diablo* and was called that by people who didn't know his name. His name is actually Luiz Garza."

"Do you know where we can find him?"

"If it's like it was on the other case, it won't be easy. You know, Berto, we had a list of seven to contact first, and we've seen four of the seven. The last one we saw was where Diablo was when we got there. I suggest we go ahead and see the other three on the list and mention Luiz when we talk to them and see their reaction when we mention his name. If we don't come up with something on the next three, then I think we should start over because I'm convinced that one or more of the seven know more than they're telling us."

"Good thinking. Let's try and get a lead on him after lunch. If we can't find anything on him this afternoon, we'll pick up on the list, where we left off, tonight."

While they were at lunch, Berto said, "Dario, do

you think the department will still have the paperwork on the 'blood atonement' case you were telling me about? If they do, then there should be some information about Luiz Garza, shouldn't there?"

"You would think so. When we get back, let's locate those files and see what we can find."

They searched and searched and finally found the files they were looking for, and they took them into an empty room and laid them on a table. They began looking through all the papers and, at last, they found some things having to do with the assailants. There were several names listed, including Luiz Garza. Upon closer examination, there were some other names listed that were the same as names on their current search list, including Angel Duran and Matzo Avila.

Berto asked Dario, "Do you recognize any other names on here, other than Luiz, Angel, and Matzo?"

"Well, when I read them, they look familiar, but I can't say I recognize any of them. As you can see, there are a lot of names here, and this crime was several years ago. I don't know how I recognized Luiz Garza. I guess maybe because he was the ringleader, and we were in touch with him more than the others."

Since the fire and the publicity it brought, many people were hoping the guilty party or parties would soon be caught, and if anyone saw or heard anything, they would call the police to report what they saw or heard. One lady in particular called in and said she saw three men at the Capo Street building the night of the fire. When asked whether or not she knew them, she said she didn't, but if she saw them again, she would recognize them. When asked for her name and address, she gave it to them, and Berto and Dario would soon take advantage of that.

While still at police headquarters, Berto asked, "Do we have photos of any of these guys?"

Dario said, "I don't know if we have any here, but you know, when somebody gets their driver's license, they have their picture made, and I feel sure the license bureau has copies."

Smiling, Berto said, "Man, Dario, you're a virtual fountain of information today. Get the list of the guys we're looking at, and let's go over to the license bureau right now."

At the license bureau, they ran into a typical government attitude. The person they talked to said they would get them the photos they wanted, but it would possibly take a week before they could get to it. Berto said, "If the head of the Bureau is here, I want to see him."

In a few minutes, a man came to where they were and said, "I understand you want a group of photocopies and want them immediately. I'm sorry, but we just can't do that. Your request has to go through our normal routine for such requests, and we are behind right now, so it will be at least next Thursday before we can get them for you."

Berto said, "Sir, you don't understand. This is a matter of national security, and we need those copies now."

"I'm sorry, Detective, but next week is the best we can do."

While still standing in the lobby of the license bureau, in the presence of the head of the bureau, Berto called Tomas Marin, the Chief of Police. When the chief answered, Berto said, "Chief, this is Berto. Dario and I are at the Driver's License Bureau trying to get some photos of some people we are pretty sure had something to do with the fire we're investigating, but they're telling us it will be at least a week before we can get them. How about calling President Putra and tell him this and see what he wants us to do. We'll wait here until we hear from you. Thanks."

Director Aguillar had an unbelievable look on his face, but he didn't say anything. In a couple of minutes, there was a page for him. The person paging him said he had a call from the president. He tried to laugh it off in order to cover his embarrassment, and he said, with an artificial smile on his face, "Everybody's a jokester." He left immediately, though, to go back to his office or somewhere to answer the phone and left Berto and Dario standing there. In about one more minute, Berto's phone rang, and it was Chief Marin. He said, "I told the president about your problem, and he's going to call the director. Maybe you won't have to wait 'til next Thursday. Let me know if you don't get what you need."

In a minute, the director came back out and said, "Detective, I talked to some of my associates, and we want to do everything we can for the police, and we'll rush your request through. It's mid-afternoon now, and we can't possibly have everything you need this afternoon, but if you will give us until ten o'clock tomorrow morning, we'll have your photos for you. Is that satisfactory?"

He never mentioned that the president had called him, and Berto didn't mention it either. He just told the director, "Yes, if that's the way it has to be, we'll just have to wait. Thank you so much. We'll see you at ten in the morning."

When they got in the car to leave, Berto said, "I guess that guy will know the next time we want something, that he needs to get on it."

"I think you're right. Do you want to go question the next guy on the list, or wait until we get the drivers license photos?"

"I think we should wait; besides, we need to talk to that witness first, anyway. I'd like to think that her witness could solve all this, and we wouldn't need to question the whole list. Maybe her word will let us narrow the list of suspects down to two or three or maybe just one."

Chapter Fifteen

Berto and Dario arrived at the license bureau at ten o'clock the next morning, and when they walked in, their photos were ready and waiting on them. They went to the car and opened the envelope they were in, and not only did they get the photos, they got other information about the men, such as their address, physical description, and date of birth.

They arranged the photos, etcetera, into the order in which they wanted to show the lady that said she would recognize the men if she saw them again. Driver's license photos are famous for being bad photos, but they hoped the pictures they had would be good enough for her to identify the men she saw.

They went back to headquarters and called her when they got there. Berto was the one who called and when she answered, he said, "Mrs. Mora, this is Detective Berto Ochoa. I understand that you might be able to identify the men who burned the church on Capo Street Monday night, and I wonder if you could come to police headquarters and talk to my partner and me. We have photos of several men, hopefully including the men you said you saw. When do you think you could come?"

She said, "I can come right after lunch, if that's alright. What did you say your name is?"

"Berto Ochoa, and my partner is Dario Barrero.

Why don't we look for you at one thirty? Is that alright?"

"Yes. I'll see you then."

After they hung up, they went into Chief Marin's office and talked about their experience at the license plate office and were amazed at how fast things moved after the president's phone call to the director. When they had talked a few more minutes, Berto and Dario grabbed a quick bite at The Speedy Taco and went back to the office to wait on Mrs. Mora to come in.

She arrived pretty close to one thirty, like she said, and Berto greeted her and directed her to a small room off the main hall, normally used for interrogations. She seemed pretty much at ease and was easy to talk to. Berto tried to make her feel at home by asking several personal questions. After they had a brief question and answer session, she said that her late husband had been a member of the Church of the First Born of the Lamb of God and what a vicious group they were. She said, "I live on Capo Street, and I was out in my yard when I saw three men drive up and get out at the building that was burned. I knew the building was used for a religious service on Sunday, and when I saw those men, I knew instantly what they were up to."

"Did you say you didn't know any of them when you called?"

"No, I didn't know any of them, but I think I can identify them if I see them again."

"Mrs. Mora, we have pictures of several men who we suspect might be connected to the fire, but before I show them to you, I'd like for you to tell us exactly what they did when they went to the building."

"Well, like I said, I was out in my yard when they pulled up, and they were pretty nonchalant as they went up to the building. One of them took something and broke the window in the front door and reached in and unlocked the door. Then, they all went in, and in just a couple of minutes, I saw smoke coming out of one of the windows. Then, right after I saw the smoke, the three came out the front door and casually walked to their car, and that's when I saw the flames. I'm the one who called the fire department, and by the time they got there, the building was about gone. That's about all I know."

"Mrs. Mora, did the men see you?"

"If they did, it didn't bother them, but I'll tell you this, Detective, it bothered me and it still does because I know what kind of people those people are. My Husband was one of them. You had better catch them before they kill somebody."

"That's exactly what we're trying to do. Let me show you some photos, and you tell me if you recognize any of them as ones who burned the building."

Instead of showing the pictures to her one by one, he decided to lay them all out on a table, so she could pick out the ones she recognized as if in a lineup. She looked them over carefully and didn't say a thing.

Then, she started over, looking at them one at a time. When she came to Angel Duran's picture, she said, "That's one of them."

Berto said, "Good, now see if you recognize anybody else." She started again, and in a minute, she picked out Alfredo Diaz, and then she came to one that she just couldn't seem to let go. Finally, she said, "This is the third man." She was looking at the picture of Luiz Garza, and she said, "We called him *El Diablo*, the devil, and he is truly a devil."

"Anybody else, Mrs. Mora?"

"No. There were just three."

"Well, thank you so much. You can't imagine how much you've helped us. We really appreciate it," and he escorted her to the door and said, "Goodbye."

They went into the Chief's office and Berto said, "We've got 'em."

Chief Marin said, "You've got 'em?"

"Yes sir. That lady that said she saw the men burn the building just left, and she identified all three. We've already questioned two of them, and we know who the third one is, but we still have to find him. Do you think we should go ahead and arrest the two we know or wait until we find the third one and arrest all of them?"

The Chief said, "I'd go ahead and arrest the two you know. It might be a while before you find the third one, and if all three are free, then you don't know what they might do in the meantime."

"Okay, Chief. We need to wait until after six to

pick them up because they work and don't get home until then."

"Great. Are you going to get them tonight?"

"I thought we would," Berto said.

"That's great. I'll stay here until you bring them in. I want to personally tell the president. Do you think we should make a poster for the third man, or do you think you're going to be able to find him?"

Dario said, "I think we'll find him. We actually saw him the other night when we went to one of the other guy's houses, but we didn't know we wanted him at the time and didn't recognize him, but you know, now that I think about it, a poster might not be such a bad idea."

Berto asked Dario, "Which one do you want to get first, Alfredo or Angel?"

"Let's get Alfredo. While we're there, I want to see the look in his wife's eyes, since she lied to us."

"Okay, are you ready?"

"I'm ready. It's seven o'clock, and he should be home by now. Let's get him."

They went to Alfredo Diaz's house and rang the doorbell. Alfredo came to the door and Berto said, "Alfredo Diaz, you're under arrest for arson. Please come with us. Just then, Alfredo's wife came into the room and asked, "What's happening here? and Alfredo said, "These idiots are arresting me for arson or some trumped up charge. Since I'm innocent, I should be out in a couple of hours, so be ready to come after me when I call you."

Dario said, "Alfredo, it's very doubtful that you'll be out in a couple of hours. Your participation in the fire of that church has put you in deep stuff, so don't look to get out anytime soon."

They took him to jail and booked him. The Magistrate set his bail at seventeen million pesos, which is almost a million dollars, American.

By then, it was ten o'clock, and they went to Angel Duran's. Angel came to the door, and Berto said, "Hi, Angel. Did you have a good day?"

He said, "Yeah, it was okay. Why are you here this late?"

Berto said, "We're sorry it's so late, but we felt we had to come tonight because you're under arrest for the arson of the church building on Capo Street last Monday night."

Angel said, "I don't know what you're talking about. What arson?"

Dario said, "Angel, put your hands behind you."

He obeyed and as soon as he had him cuffed, he asked, "Angel, we're looking for your buddy, Luiz. Do you know exactly where he lives?"

Angel asked, "Who?"

"Luiz Garza, the guy who was here Wednesday night when we came to see you."

"I don't know who you're talking about. I don't know any Luiz Garza."

They took him to jail, and the Magistrate set his bail the same as Alfredo's; seventeen million pesos.

By then, it was almost midnight, so the detectives

went home and got a good night's sleep, anxious to get a running start the next day, looking for Luiz, *El Diablo,* Garza.

The next morning, they took the driver's license picture of Luiz Garza to a printer and ordered a large amount of posters to display on the whole island.

Chief Marin was very happy to have two of the three arsonists in jail, and he called President Putra to tell him the good news, and just as soon as they hung up, President Putra called Monty Shepherd.

When Monty answered, President Putra said, "Good morning, Monty. Arin."

"Good morning, Arin. How are you this morning?"

"Excellent. I've got some news for you. It's what I'd say is semi good news, and hopefully, by the end of the day we can take the semi off."

"Great. What is it?"

"Well, the police found out that three men were involved in the fire, and as of last night, we have two of them in jail, and we know who the third man is. He is the ringleader, and he's slick. He's known as *El Diablo*, the Devil. His real name is Luiz Garza."

"Did you say Luiz Garza?"

"Yes sir."

"Arin, I know a Luiz Garza. He works for us at the plant, in fact, Bimo has been training him to be plant manager. I'm getting ready to go to the plant, now, and if he's there, I'll call Chief Marin."

"Good, and call me, too, will you?"

"I certainly will. Man, that's some coincidence, isn't it?"

"It sure is. I'll listen for your call."

He hurried and got ready and headed to the plant. As soon as he got there, he looked up Bimo. When he found him, he asked, "Bimo, is Luiz Garza here this morning?"

"No sir. Luiz hasn't been here in two days and hasn't called. I don't know what to think because I have been training him to be plant manager. If you don't mind me asking, why are you interested in Luiz?"

"Because an eyewitness has identified him as one of three men who burned our church. The other two are in jail. Do you know where he lives?"

"Not exactly. I heard him say that he lives down on Front Street, close to the docks."

"Get his personnel file, and let's see what it shows for his address."

Bimo went in the office and told one of the women, who did the payroll, to get the file for Luiz Garza. She took it out of the cabinet and handed it to him. He held it where he and Monty could both see it, and it showed his address as 203 Front Street.

"Do you know where that is?" Monty asked.

"I know where Front Street is, but I'm not sure about 203. Luiz told me one time that he lived with a woman on the second floor over some kind of business."

"Well, we need to call this information in to the

police," Monty said. "Do you know the number of the police department?"

"No sir, but I can find it."

He looked through some kind of directory and wrote down a number. He gave it to Monty and said, "Here it is."

Monty dialed the number and when someone answered on the other end, he said, "Chief Marin, please. This is Monty Shepherd."

It was only a few seconds until Chief Marin answered. "Hi Monty. What's up?"

"I understand you're looking for Luiz Garza, and I have his address, in case you don't have it."

"Fantastic. Hold on and let me get something to write on." In about five seconds, he said, "Okay. Shoot," and he wrote it down as Monty called it out to him. "This is great. How did you get this, Monty?"

"Would you believe he has been working for me here at the plant?"

The Chief asked, "Is he there now?"

"No, and Bimo said he hasn't shown up for work since Tuesday, so I don't know where he is, but I'll bet you can find him."

"I hope we can. Thanks, Monty."

He spent another hour or so at the plant and then went back to the hotel, where Joan was. He went to the room and told her, "Come on and go with me. I want to go somewhere and try to find something". She didn't question him. She just grabbed her bag and followed him to the elevator. When they got in the car, she asked, "Where are we going?"

"I'm not sure," he said. I want to try to find an address."

He wasn't sure exactly where Front Street was, but he knew it was close to the boat docks, and he knew the ocean was south of where they were, so he turned the Suburban to the left until the compass showed he was heading south. He stayed in that direction until he came to the ocean. When he reached the ocean, he turns right and drove up the ocean street until he saw a road sign that read FRONT ST. He told Joan to look for numbers on the buildings until they came to 203, and when they got near to the 200 block, there were police cars parked out front, and he wondered if they were able to catch Luiz. He didn't stop. He was just curious about where Luiz lived. They went back to the hotel and changed into their beachwear and went to the beach.

Soon, after they had settled into some comfortable chaise lounges, Monty's phone rang. The voice on the other end said, "Monty, Tomas Marin here. I sent some officers to the Front Street address you gave me, but Luiz Garza had gone. The unit at two o three is rented to a Camila Mendez, and she is supposedly the girlfriend of Garza. She is a second shift waitress at The Green Cactus, and we're going to try and see her there after she gets to work.

Joan was good to not ask too many questions, she pretty much left it up to Monty to tell her things whenever he thought she should know them. He had been very busy with trying to get the church started and then the church burning, and now the manhunt, and he had told her surprisingly little. He got to thinking about that, and while they were relaxed on the beach, he thought that would be a good time to bring her up to date on what had been happening.

Chief Marin's phone call triggered the thought, so he turned over toward her and said, "That was the police chief saying the guy they're looking for was not at the Front Street location where we went earlier. He said the unit at two o three is rented to Luiz's girlfriend. She's a waitress and will be going to work at three o'clock this afternoon, and they're going to try and see her there."

Joan asked, "Now, who is Luiz?"

"Remember me telling you there were three men that burned our building? Well, they caught two of them and Luiz is the third. Do you know what name a lot of people call him?"

"No, what?"

"They call him *El Diablo*, the Devil, because he is so ruthless, and Honey, would you believe he has been working for us at the plant? It's kind of ironic; there I was, trying to do things for God, and not knowing I was employing the devil. I just hope his girlfriend will help the police. Even though they've caught the other two, if *El Diablo* is allowed to remain free, then with his influence, it shouldn't be hard for him to recruit others to help him do other things, maybe harm some of our people."

"Honey, what does he have against religion? Why does he do these things?"

"I won't get into the background, but there is, or was, a powerful Mormon cult that was vicious. The heads of the cult believed that if you crossed them, you would be guilty of sinning, and you would have to be punished by what they called 'blood atonement'. 'Blood atonement' required bloodshed or even murder to pay for sinning against the cult leader. The cult is supposedly no longer in existence, but there are many people in San Sorento that are still followers, including Luiz Garza, and their very mention of his name brings fear to those who still believe." After he told her about the FBL and Luiz, they talked about other things, and when the conversation slowed, they both took a nap.

They had been asleep for about a half hour when Monty's phone woke them up. When he answered, it was Chief Marin. "Monty. Tomas. We talked to Camila Mendez, this afternoon, and she denied that Luiz Garza is her boyfriend. She said that he is actually homeless, and she felt sorry for him and let him stay at her place for a couple of days. We knew she was lying by the way she talked, so we're going to stake her place out, day and night for a while. We're pretty sure he'll turn up there sooner or later."

"Well, I appreciate you calling, Tomas. I hope it's sooner, rather than later because I need to go home, and I don't feel like I can as long as that dude is on the loose."

"We'll get him, and Monty, I think it will be sooner. I'll let you know when I hear something."

"Thank you, Tomas. Bye."

He told Joan, "That was the Chief of Police, and they still haven't caught Luiz. Are you hungry?"

"I'm starved."

"Where would you like to eat?"

"Anywhere you'd like."

"What would you like?"

"You know what? I'd love some good fresh fried Scallops."

"That's interesting I was just told about a place that has good scallops."

"What is it? Is it close?"

"It's called El Marinero. It sounds Italian, but they say the seafood is wonderful. Everything is fresh from the ocean each day."

"Good. Let's go there. I hope it's good."

The El Marinero was located at the north end of Front Street, the street they went to that morning, looking for the place they thought was where Luiz was staying. They went in and the atmosphere was typical seafood restaurant. Joan was looking for scallops and the waitress said, "I normally don't like seafood, but the scallops are like eating candy, they're so good."

Joan and Monty, both ordered them, and while they were waiting, Bimo and Sofia came in. When they saw each other, Monty invited them to sit with them, and they did. Not much was said while they read the menu, and Bimo asked, "What are you all having?"

Joan answered, "We're having scallops. Somebody told Monty that they're real good."

Then Bimo said, "I'll have scallops, too." He looked at Sofia and asked, "What about you?"

"She said, "I guess I'll have them, too. I love scallops."

They ordered and then the conversation began. Monty began it by smiling and saying, "This is about the third or fourth place where we've run into you guys. You must like each other's company."

Bimo said, "We do, and that's not all."

"What do you mean"? Monty asked.

Bimo and Sofia looked at each other and smiled, then Bimo said, "We're talking about getting married. But there are some major obstacles standing in our way."

"I can see that," Monty said. "One of you lives here and one in Chattanooga. If you get married, one of you will have to move, won't you? You don't have to be a brain surgeon to know that's a major obstacle. Have you thought about what you're going to do?"

Sofia said, "We've talked about it a lot, and I don't see how it can work, but Bimo seems to think there will be a way. Maybe you can help us with a solution. Can you?"

Monty said, "Oh no. Leave me out of this. I have enough problems already. You're both smart, and I'm sure you'll figure it out."

"We don't mean to burden you with our problems, Monty, but whatever we decide to do is going to affect you in some way because we both work for you. I feel like I'm one of your key people, especially here in San Sorento, and Sofia is doing more and more and might be considered a key employee, so if you have any ideas, we would sure like to hear them."

They brought the food and everyone dug in. Monty, however, didn't go at it with the enthusiasm that the others did because his conversation with Bimo and Sofia sort of curbed his appetite. He wanted to change the subject, so he asked Bimo, "Bimo, how well do you know Luiz Garza?"

"Well, I thought I knew him better than I do. One time, before you came here, he applied for a job with us, and I liked him and thought he would make a good plant manager, so I hired him. He worked for a while, and then, all at once, he failed to show up for work for three days without calling or otherwise letting us know why he was absent, so I fired him, and I haven't seen him for two or three years.

"Then, when word got out that Shepherd Apparel was going to reopen the San Sorento Clothing plant, he came in one day and asked me for a job. He apologized for the way he did earlier and made some questionable excuses, but I still like him, and I hired him to come in and be trained as the plant manager like before. That's all I know."

"Did you know that he was involved with the First Born cult?"

"No sir. I had no idea."

"Did you ever hear anybody call him *El Diablo*?"

"You know, I did hear somebody call him that one time, but I just thought they were joking. Now I know better."

They finished eating and talked for a little while longer, and then Monty picked up the check for all four, and they all left.

On the way back to the hotel, Joan asked, "Honey, isn't there some way you can help those two?"

"How? They live two thousand miles apart. If they both lived here or both in Chattanooga, then maybe I could do something, but the way it is, I'll have to say there are going to be two brokenhearted people."

She asked, "Since they both work for you, couldn't you transfer one of them to where the other one lives?

"I don't know if that's the answer. Bimo has lived here his whole life and Sofia has lived in Chattanooga since she was a little girl, and her whole family is there. Bimo probably won't leave, and I doubt if Sofia will. It's just something they're going to have to work out. I thought, in the beginning, that the Chattanooga people would be here for around six months, but the way things are developing, it looks as if six months is turning into three or three and a half months. When I send them all back home, I guess Sofia will go with them, and while it will be hard for them for a while, it should solve their problem."

"I hope so. I feel sorry for them."

Chapter Twenty

Joan's concern for Sofia and Bimo touched Monty, and he thought he might try to help them in some way. Since the next day was Saturday, and nobody had to work, he thought that might be a good time to talk to them, so he called Bimo and asked if he and Sofia would like to come over to the hotel and spend some time on the beach with him and Joan, so they could talk about some things.

Bimo jumped at the chance, and he and Sofia went over shortly after lunch the way Monty suggested, and since the wind was pretty strong that day, they sat around the pool instead of the beach. They talked about the usual unimportant things such as the weather, the way things went at work that week, and the arrest of the two arsonists.

Then, Monty asked, "Have you two figured out what you're going to do yet?"

Bimo said, "No, and we're starting to get worried about it."

"Sofia, I'm sure you have had many thoughts about it. Why don't you tell me some of them?"

"Monty, as we've already told you, neither one of us wants to leave our home, but we want to get married and live together. I've had one thought, but it involves you or Shepherd Apparel, and I hate to mention it."

"Go ahead and tell me, Sofia. We're just talking this afternoon, and I want to hear your ideas, so tell me what your thought is."

"Okay, but I don't want you to get mad at me."

"I'm not going to get mad at you. Tell me whatever you want."

"Alright." She looked at Bimo with what looked like fear on her face and said. "I've been thinking that maybe Bimo and I could get married, and I could move over here and live with him, and maybe, since the supply plane comes over here once a week, maybe I could catch a ride on it and go home once every two or three months. I could go home on one trip and then, when it comes back the next week, I could ride it back."

"That sounds pretty good, but I can see some problems with it. If I give you free transportation and a week off every two or three months, what if other employees would want the same deal?"

"Well, by then, all the Chattanooga employees will be back home, and the only one left over here will be me. I'm pretty sure none of the San Sorentoans would want to do that. Also, Monty, if you would let me do this, I would be glad to sign an agreement saying that I would not be considered a full time employee, and you could pay me strictly piece work rates with no hourly wage involved, unless I was pulled off hemming to train someone, and then you could pay me hourly for the time I spend training. That way, I would be considered an outside contractor, and you wouldn't have to give me any of the Shepherd Apparel benefits. Bimo would receive the benefits, and I would get what other family members of employees get."

Monty said, "Boy, you really have been doing a lot of thinking. What do you think about that, Bimo?"

"I think she is very smart to come up with that idea. She has told me about another idea that she hasn't mentioned to you."

"What is it, Sofia?"

"Well, I'm almost afraid to mention it, but I would like for you to let Bimo and me ride to Chattanooga on the plane, so we can get married in Chattanooga, and then the following week, we can come back on that week's plane, unless, of course, you would like for us to stay for two weeks so we could have a honeymoon."

Monty laughed and said, "You aren't asking for much, are you, young lady?"

She said, "Well, you said for me to tell you what I've been thinking, and that's what I've been thinking, and I really don't expect you to do it, but that's what I would hope and pray for."

"Your request is very unusual, and I'm not saying we can't do it, but I am saying, I need to think about it and let you know. I do have one question, and that is, what will you do for a car if you move over here?"

"Well, I've thought about that, too. If we're both working, we will probably be able to afford to buy a car. You're already furnishing one to Bimo, and we can get by with that if we have to. I have a car in Chattanooga that I can use if I get to go home every once in a while."

"Sofia, I admire you for such in depth thinking. Maybe we can do something that will make both of us happy. Now that we've discussed that, I want to tell you all something. Things are going so well at the plant, now, and most everybody knows what they're doing, and the trainers are just sort of spinning their wheels, I'm thinking that I can let just about all the Chattanooga folks go home in another month or six weeks. I had originally thought that it might take as long as six months to get everybody trained, but it looks as though three months is going to be enough. The timing for this hits you guys just right, doesn't it?"

Soon, they stopped talking about what was going to or not going to happen, and they were all pretty much out of something to talk about. Monty thought that they must have thought he meant for them to come over and spend the day because when they finished talking about the possible wedding, Bimo and Sofia got up and ran down to the beach and into the ocean despite the wind. When they got out, they came back up to the pool and stretched out on the chaise lounges they had been sitting on. He and Joan looked at each other and smiled, but they didn't say anything.

After they had been there for about four or five hours, it was approaching six o'clock, and Joan said,

"I'm hungry. Is anybody else hungry?"

"Bimo said, "I'm starving. I didn't have any lunch."

Monty took the hints and asked, "Would you all like to go get a hamburger?"

They all said they would, so they went to the Pueblo and ate. When they returned to the hotel, Sofia and Bimo didn't come in. They said they had to go. Monty figured they had plans, since it was Saturday night. They both thanked him and Joan for the afternoon and for the burgers, and they left.

Monty's phone was ringing when he opened the door to their room, and it was Tomas Marin, the Chief of Police. "Monty, Tomas Marin. How are you doing?"

"I'm great, Tomas. What's happening?"

"We got him, Monty."

"Luiz Garza?"

"Yes sir. Our men saw him trying to get on the ferry to Isla Fibulon, and they arrested him without any resistance. He's in jail now, with his buddies and hopefully, that's where he'll stay for a long time."

"Fantastic. Congratulations, Tomas. Thank you so much for calling. This will be something good to tell in church, in the morning."

"It sure will. I'm anxious to see people's faces when you tell them."

Monty asked, "Would you like to tell them, Tomas?"

"Oh no. I'm not a speaker. I'll let you tell them,

and I'll just watch their faces."

"Okay, if that's what you want. So you'll be there in the morning?"

"Yes. My wife said we should join your group, so yes, we'll be there."

"Great. I'll look for you. Thanks again, Tomas."

"You're welcome."

He hung up and told Joan, excitingly, "Honey, they caught Diablo."

"Really? That's wonderful."

"It sure is."

He told her, "Remind me in the morning to call Bimo. I need for him to help me with something tomorrow at church."

He was so excited about the police catching Luiz Garza that he called Jimmy to tell him. Soon, after he answered, he said, "Dad, I was just about to call you. A few weeks ago, you asked me to try to find someone to be a missionary to San Sorento, and I think I might have found one. After you told me that you needed someone, I talked to Pastor Darrell, and he called me yesterday, and he said he knows a man who he thinks would fit in perfectly for what you're wanting, and one of the best parts is this guy speaks fluent Spanish. I was going to ask you if you wanted me to try to get this guy to catch our plane next week and then speak at your church next Sunday for a trial sermon.

"After he preaches the trial, you all can decide whether or not you want to hire him, and if you do, you will be free to come home. Monty hadn't even had a chance to tell Jimmy about the capture of *El Diablo*, and when he did, Jimmy said, "All the better. Now you won't have to worry about getting burned out or maybe killed. All you'll have to think about is connecting the people of San Sorento to God. If he can come next week, do you want me to send him on our plane?"

"If you think he's the one, it'll be okay, I guess."

"I don't know the guy, Dad, but Pastor Darrell says he's one of the most dynamic preachers he's ever heard, and it seems to me, that that's what you need out there. I thought after I spoke with Darrell, that God sure does work in mysterious ways, because six months ago, you had never heard of San Sorento, and now, He's sending someone to step in take over a base that you have and are setting up for Him, and the two of you will help save a population that, for the most part, has never even heard of Him."

Monty said, "I haven't thought about it that way, but I guess you're right. This place is potentially wide open to hear about the Lord, and maybe this guy is the guy to do it. Go ahead and send him if he will come, and we'll see what happens."

"Oh, by the way, Dad, I wasn't able to get the second order of Bibles on the last plane, so they will be there on the next one, and oh yeah, that missionary is named Jack Vernon."

After he hung up, he bowed his head and thanked God for seeing that the Devil was captured. Now, maybe there won't be anymore burning or any other kinds of terrorism having to do with their new church. He also thanked God for maybe sending them a missionary to carry on His work, and finally, he asked God to help them find a permanent church building where they can freely worship.

He then studied his notes on the remarks he was going to make the next morning, and after studying for a little while, he went to bed and slept like a baby until the next morning.

He and Joan got up early Sunday morning, had some coffee in their room and then, when Joan got ready, they went downstairs for breakfast. He called Bimo at eight o'clock, and when Bimo saw who was calling he answered with, "Good morning, Monty."

Monty said, "Hey Bimo. Listen, I need for you to do something for me this morning. I need for you to go by the plant and pick up a two-wheel hand truck and meet me at the Capitol with it at nine thirty. Can you do that?"

"I can. Do you need anything else?"

"No. That's all. Thanks."

He and Joan went back upstairs after breakfast and finished getting ready for church. They left for the Capitol at nine o'clock to meet Bimo at nine thirty.

Bimo was right on time, and he wanted to know what to do with the hand truck. Monty called him over to the Suburban and asked him to load some boxes and push them into the room where their meeting would be held. There were eight boxes, and none of them were extra heavy, but if one tried to hand carry them the long way from the parking lot to the conference room, it would be a really hard job, so the hand truck saved the day.

Inside, they emptied the boxes of Bibles on to a table and separated the English from the Spanish translations. He didn't take the songbooks in because he thought without a piano or guitar, it would be hard for them to sing.

When it looked as if everyone was seated, Monty stood up and addressed the group. He thanked everybody for being there, and he pointed out that that was the largest group they had had yet. Nearly all the Chattanooga people were there, plus it looked as if maybe seventy-five San Sorentoans were there also.

Before he started his remarks, he wanted to make a couple or three announcements, and he began by offering each person a Bible. Pointing out that some of them were in English and some in Spanish. He told them that there would be more next Sunday in case they didn't get one.

Next, he talked about the suppression and persecution they had suffered up to that point, and he thanked God that the persecutors had been caught. He called Luiz Garza by name and said that many people called him *El Diablo*, or Devil. He said that Garza had been working for him at the plant, and he thought it was ironic that he was trying to do God's work, and the whole time, the Devil was working for him. He told the people how glad he was that the three were caught and how glad he was that they were going to have to go to prison, but at the same time, he asked everybody there to pray for them.

Finally, in his announcements, he talked about the possibility of another person coming to lead them in their quest to find Jesus. He pointed out that the man could speak fluent Spanish, and it would be easier for them to understand him because there wouldn't have to be a separate interpreter, then when the Chattanooga people left, the entire group would be Spanish speaking, and it would really be better. He hoped he would be there in time to speak to them next Sunday, and to please remember the name of Jack Vernon.

Then he said, "Oh yeah, I almost forgot. Can anyone in here play the piano?" No one raised their hand. "Well, can anyone in here play the guitar?" and several hands went up, and he said to those who raised their hands, "Good. If any of you who raised your hands would be interested in playing two or three songs each week for our service, would you please see me up here right after this morning's service?"

Then he began his remarks and read from the Gospel of John and delivered a very powerful message, and at the end, when he issued an invitation to accept Christ, twenty-six people went forward, most of them San Sorentoans, including Tomas and Rosa Marin, the Chief of Police and his wife.

Word was getting around San Sorento about the FBL terrorists' arrest and upcoming trial, and there was almost a nationwide sense of relief. People were more relaxed, and it seemed as though fear was replaced with happiness, and Monty attributed the large turnout for church to that. He hoped that when more people were made aware of it that church attendance would really grow.

On Thursday, the supply plane came in, and Jack Vernon was on it. Monty was there to meet the plane and he gave thanks for Jack coming. After they unloaded the Bibles, they went to the Holiday Shores, where Monty checked him into a room. He liked Jack right away and was anxious to see how he behaved in front of a crowd of people and how he preached. Jack looked to be about Jimmy's age, and he told Monty that he was married and had two small children, both home schooled by his wife, so there wouldn't be a problem with education in case he came there on a permanent basis.

Monty and Joan spent quite a bit of time with him the rest of the day, Thursday, and then on Friday and Saturday, they took him around and showed him San Sorento, in between trips to the pool and the beach. On Saturday afternoon, he told Monty that if he was going to speak Sunday morning, that he needed some time to work on his talk, so Monty left him alone all afternoon with the promise to take him to dinner whenever he called and said he was ready.

Sunday services just kept growing in attendance,

and the next day, there were just about all of the Chattanooga folks plus over a hundred local people who were now not afraid to come out and worship God. After everyone was seated, Monty stood up and made a few remarks, and then, he introduced Jack Vernon, who thanked him and began his remarks. The crowd was anxious to hear him as was Monty because he wanted to be sure the person he turned over the responsibility of introducing San Sorento to Jesus was the right person.

Jack began by saying how glad he was to be there, and he wanted to talk to them for a few minutes about God's messengers. He asked, "Do you know what an angel is?" and nobody reacted, and he went on to say that the Bible talks about angels, and that they can take different forms. Angels are usually defined as God's messengers.

He said, "This morning I want to talk about one of God's messengers, who I think you know," and he went on to tell them about how six months ago, practically no one in San Sorento even knew who God was, and then by chance two couples came there on vacation, and a local man approached one of the men with something of interest to him, and long story short, that man not only resurrected a dying business in San Sorento, but he fought through persecution and suppression to introduce a few people to God. In my opinion, that man is an angel or God's messenger. His name is Monty Shepherd, and without his efforts and perseverance, none of you would be here this morning, and you need to thank God for sending you Monty." He went on and told a couple of stories about angels, and then wound up his remarks. He invited anybody who would like to become a child of God to come forward, and thirty-three people went forward, all of them from San Sorento. Before he dismissed, he asked everybody to invite their family and friends to come next week.

Six or seven people met Monty after the service and said they would be willing to play their guitars, so people could sing. He took their names and told them that someone would be in touch and set things up with them.

After they left, he went over to Jack and shook his hand and said, "Great job. I think you can see that these people are hungry for the Lord. If you decide you want to come here, I'll give you all the support I can, and we'll start getting things set up for you. And oh, yeah, when you were meeting some of the people after your message, do you happen to remember a nice couple named Putra? His name is Arin, and his wife's name is Juanita."

"Yeah, I remember them. They were very impressive. Why do you ask?"

"Because Arin is the president of San Sorento. In public, you should call him Mr. President. Just so you'll know."

"Thanks, Monty."

Jack told Monty that he felt he should come here and would be anxious to start working with the local people. They went to lunch, and then back to the hotel, where they talked at length about some of the things that had to be done in order for him to come full time. First on the list was a place for him and his family to live, then, there was the problem of getting all his furniture and two automobiles moved. Of course, Monty would be a big help. More than likely, he would move the furniture and cars on the C-130 as well as Jack and his wife and children.

Number one was to find a place to live, and Monty called on Bimo to help with the house search. In turn, Bimo called on some of his friends to help, and it only took a few days before the perfect place was found. It had three bedrooms, two bathrooms, a den and kitchen, and it was within walking distance of the beach. The rent was very reasonable, and Jack was very happy to get it.

The next supply plane came on Thursday, and Jack returned to Chattanooga on it when it went back Friday. He had a lot to tell when he got back. His leaving meant Monty would have to stay at least one more week because attendance had increased so much, he was a little afraid to leave it in the hands of Bill Glasser, although Bill might be able to handle it.

He called Jimmy and told him about Jack and how well he did. He told him that Jack wanted to come to San Sorento full time, and he asked Jimmy to call Pastor Darrell to see if they could get Jack's mission job turned over to the Mission Board. He thought he would foot the bill for everything, if he had to, but if they could get the Mission Board to take it over, all the better.

Four weeks later

Jack and his family were settled in, and Jack had preached three times after he moved, and the attendance each week was increasing as was the number of decisions for Christ. It looked as though the Mission Board was going to adopt him as a missionary, but in the meantime, Monty was footing all the bills, including his salary.

The trials for the three church arsonists had just been completed. Alfredo Diaz and Angel Duran were tried together, and they each received an eight-year sentence.

Luiz Garza was tried alone, and as leader of the now defunct cult, he was sentenced to ten years.

The San Sorento government had an agreement with the Mexican government whereby convicted prisoners in San Sorento would serve their sentences, if over five years in a Mexican penitentiary. Alfredo and Angel were both ordered to spend their time at the prison in Baja, California, Mexico and Luiz was sent to Colonia Juarez, Chihuahua.

Three Weeks Later

Monty decided that the Shepherd employees from Chattanooga had done an excellent job of training and retraining the employees at San Sorento, so he called off the six month assignment after thirteen weeks, a little over three months. He had pushed Pablo Sanchez, the manager of the Dunes Resort, so hard to get the rent down for six months, that he felt bad leaving after only three, so he went to Pablo and told him they were pulling out, but he would pay him the same as if they were all still there. He did, however, work out a deal with him to hold three efficiencies vacant from then on, for his pilots that came in at least once a week. This thrilled Pablo, and he was happy to do it.

Monty had agreed to Sofia's wishes about becoming an independent contractor, and her family in Chattanooga was making most of her wedding arrangements according to her instructions on the phone nearly every night. She and Bimo were on the first plane, that took half the Chattanooga employees back home, and their wedding was to take place the following week in the Basilica of Saints Peter and Paul that Sofia belonged to. Monty had relented and told them they could have two weeks before going back to San Sorento, so they could have a honeymoon.

Six Months Later

The hassle of reopening a large clothing manufacturing factory, and at the same time trying to do the will of God really beat Monty down, but things have smoothed out, finally.

After the disappointing end to Luiz Garza's short run as plant manager, Bimo and Monty got their heads together and promoted Maria Reyes from Senior Sewing Supervisor to Plant Manager.

Sometimes when a woman is made boss over other women, a problem is created, but in that case, everyone in the plant seemed to love Maria, and she was doing a great job. In fact, she had increased production to a surprisingly high figure; twelve percent over the quota set for her, so things were good at Shepherd Apparel/San Sorento.

Bimo and Sofia had now been married for about six months, and they seemed very happy. No little ones in sight yet. At their ages, there might not be any.

Shortly before Monty, Joan, and the Martins went on vacation to San Sorento, San Sorento had built a new, fairly large school, and had abandoned the old one. With the entry of Jack Vernon as pastor of the Shepherd Church, attendance was soaring, and while the facilities at the capitol were still adequate, it was easy to see that it wouldn't be long until they would need a larger place.

Since the conversion of President Putra, he has been using his influence for the Lord as much as he could. He could easily see that the church was outgrowing the Capitol, so one day, as he was passing by the abandoned school building, a light went off in his brain, and he thought that that would be a great place to hold church services. The school was owned by the State, and since he was president, he felt like he had enough influence to push the idea through. Besides, Guido Vasquez, Chief of the Legislature was also a church attending Christian, and the president felt sure that the two of them could wrangle their way to enable the church to be able to hold services there.

The school had a nice size auditorium and also a large gymnasium. The president thought that the auditorium would be large enough until they outgrew it, and then they could move into the gym. He didn't think he would be able to get the government to do any of the refurbishing, but there were now enough church members to do the job, if somebody would suggest it to them. That somebody turned out to be Bimo Flores, and one Sunday, after the government's permission was given, he stood up and announced that the government was going to let them use the school, but it needed a lot of repairs, and that very day, he recruited enough volunteers to do the work. After three or four months, those volunteers along with several new members who volunteered, had the school looking like a new one, and they were ready to move in.

Bimo, President Putra, and Chief Marin were the unofficial, recognized leaders of the church, and before the building was completely finished, the three of them met with Jack Vernon, and thought it would be appropriate to invite Monty to the grand opening and first service. He had kept in close touch through Jack and Bimo, even though he had been back in Chattanooga since before they found the school, and after the meeting of the four, Jack called to invite him, and of course, he accepted.

After he accepted the invitation to the first service in the new, old building, he thought that since Jimmy and Joan were in on starting the church from the beginning, it would be good if they were there for the first service. In fact, he thought it would be nice if his whole family was there, so he called them and asked them to go with him to San Sorento on the set date. They would take the 767 for comfort.

On the day they arrived in San Sorento, it looked sort of like a Shepherd invasion. Not only were Monty and Joan there, but Jimmy and Analisa, along with Analisa's son, Johnny. Monty's daughter, Mary Ann, was there for the first time. She was so proud of her daddy. Unfortunately, her husband couldn't come because he was holding a revival at another church.

They arrived on Saturday for the service the next morning, and there wasn't much time to show Mary Ann and Johnny anything except the beach at the hotel, but they loved it.

The next morning, Bimo and Sofia came by to lead them to the school as well as to offer them a couple more seats just in case the Suburban couldn't hold them all. When they got to the school, Monty was overwhelmed when he saw all the people coming in. Bimo led them down to the front row, where they had reserved enough seats for the family, as well as the pilots, Alex and Cody.

The service began with three men playing guitars and leading the congregation in two songs, then Jack stood up and welcomed everyone, and told them how thankful he was for being able to be there and to be able to lead them on their journey to Christ. Then he told the people about Monty and what he had done to start the church, and then he asked him to come up and say a few words. When he got up, the crowd gave him a standing ovation that lasted about a minute and a half.

He thanked them for the warm welcome and then spent a few minutes telling them how God must have led him to San Sorento. Even though Jack was fluent in Spanish, he wasn't quite as good as a native, so they had Bimo come up and interpret what he said. He spoke for five to ten minutes, telling them the important things on the journey from tourist to business owner to God's representative. He emphasized that each person there should set an example for their neighbor and if they did, then he was sure the church would grow to do unimaginable things in and for San Sorento, and then he sat down. Again, a standing ovation.

After the service, there was a taco lunch with every kind of taco imaginable, and it seemed as if everybody who had attended the service that morning was there. The Shepherds sort of hung with Jack, Bimo, the president and others who could speak English, and they stayed until everybody had gone, except for the ones they were talking with.

About mid-afternoon, they boarded the 767 and headed back to Chattanooga, and after all the talk about what Monty had done over the past several months, and all the talk about how proud each of them was of him, he looked at Joan and said, "I'm ready to go to Florida. When we get home, I want you to call Tracy Martin and see when she and Jerry can go down. San Sorento was extremely rewarding, but I'm ready to be with people that I can understand and that can understand me."